It was eight o'clock. The man on the radio told me. Then he told me about candidate Paul Abingdon again. He told me about the pictures of a sexual nature. Then he told me about the reporter for the *New York Star*. The reporter who was now believed to be John Wells.

"Shut up," I said. I killed the radio. I killed the air-conditioning. I killed the light. I plugged in the phone. It started ringing. I killed the phone. I turned my back on it and walked away.

I went to the door and opened it. The heat hit me in the face like a fist.

Then a fist hit me in the face like the heat. It was a fist the size of a basketball. A black pit opened in my head. I stumbled backward and fell into it.

from
The Rain

Coming Soon,
Keith Peterson's
Most Exciting Novel Yet:
The Scarred Man

Bantam Books offers the finest in classic and modern American murder mysteries. Ask your bookseller for the books you have missed.

Rex Stout
Broken Vase
Death of a Dude
Death Times Three
Fer-de-Lance
The Final Deduction
Gambit
The Rubber Band
Too Many Cooks
The Black Mountain

Max Allan Collins
The Dark City

A. E. Maxwell
Just Another Day in Paradise
Gatsby's Vineyard
The Frog and the Scorpion

Joseph Louis
Madelaine
The Trouble with Stephanie

M. J. Adamson
Not Till a Hot January
A February Face
Remember March

Conrad Haynes
Bishop's Gambit, Declined
Perpetual Check

Barbara Paul
First Gravedigger
But He Was Already Dead When I
   Got There

P. M. Carlson
Murder Unrenovated
Rehearsal for Murder

Ross Macdonald
The Goodbye Look
Sleeping Beauty
The Name Is Archer
The Drowning Pool
The Underground Man
The Zebra-Striped Hearse
The Ivory Grin

Margaret Maron
The Right Jack
Baby Doll Games
One Coffee With
coming soon: Corpus Christmas

William Murray
When The Fat Man Sings

Robert Goldsborough
Murder in E Minor
Death on Deadline
The Bloodied Ivy

Sue Grafton
"A" Is for Alibi
"B" Is for Burglar
"C" Is for Corpse
"D" Is for Deadbeat

Joseph Telushkin
The Unorthodox Murder of Rabbi
   Wahl
The Final Analysis of Doctor Stark

Richard Hilary
Snake in the Grasses
Pieces of Cream
Pillow of the Community

Carolyn G. Hart
Design for Murder
Death on Demand
Something Wicked
Honeymoon with Murder

Lia Matera
Where Lawyers Fear to Tread
A Radical Departure
The Smart Money
Hidden Agenda

Robert Crais
The Monkey's Raincoat

Keith Peterson
The Trapdoor
There Fell a Shadow

David Handler
The Man Who Died Laughing
coming soon: The Man Who Lived
   by Night

Marilyn Wallace
Primary Target

THE RAIN

KEITH PETERSON

BANTAM BOOKS

TORONTO · NEW YORK · LONDON · SYDNEY · AUCKLAND

THE RAIN

A Bantam Book / January 1989

ISBN 0-553-27663-8

Published simultaneously in the United States and Canada

Bantam Books are published by Bantam Books, a division of Bantam Doubleday Dell Publishing Group, Inc. Its trademark, consisting of the words "Bantam Books" and the portrayal of a rooster, is Registered in U.S. Patent and Trademark Office and in other countries. Marca Registrada, Bantam Books, 666 Fifth Avenue, New York, New York 10103

PRINTED IN THE UNITED STATES OF AMERICA

O   0 9 8 7 6 5 4 3 2 1

This book is for Glenn Borin.

1

His name was Mayforth Kendrick III. He was a weasel. He'd phoned me that afternoon at the *Star*. "Come up and see my new place, Wells," he'd said. It was August. The city was dead. He had something to sell for certain. That night, around eleven, I went to find out what it was.

His new place was on Seventh Street, off Avenue A. Half of the street's south side was taken up by an empty lot, a little rubble garden where a building had been razed. The north side of the street was a row of stoops and brick walls and dark windows. I parked the Artful Dodge on the avenue and started walking.

It was hot. The air was thick. The moisture in it turned to mist on the pavement. The mist hung low in the night. It gave the street lamps halos. It blocked out what the street lamps left of the stars. The sky was heavy with it, but it would not break and rain.

I felt like I was packed in cotton. I had my jacket over my shoulder and my tie loosened, and still my shirt clung to me, gray with sweat. My cigarette turned sour between my lips. I tossed it into the gutter.

I walked by the doorways. Dark eyes watched me go. Faces in the shadows of hat brims puckered at me. The lips hissed, "Sssmoke. Sssmoke." I kept walking. I reached Kendrick's building. A man in a khaki shirt was leaning against the stoop railing. He smiled broadly.

"He-ey." He drew the word out.

I looked at him. He stopped smiling. I trotted up the steps to the front door.

I pushed into the vestibule. The buzzers there had been torn out. That was all right: the lock was busted anyway. I pushed the inner door open. A long flight of stairs rose from the peeling linoleum of the floor. I started up.

The hot, heavy air came up with me, like I was dragging it up after me on a rope. I was breathless by the time I reached the second-floor landing. I came around the banister and walked down a hallway of anonymous black doors. Another flight of stairs. I climbed them slowly. My shoes made a sorry scraping noise as they shuffled from step to step.

My forehead streamed with sweat. I reached the third floor. I walked straight ahead to the end of the hall. The ceiling light was out. The far door was in darkness. I stepped into the darkness and knocked once.

The door swung in a little. A sickeningly sweet incense drifted out. Kendrick peeked at me over a chain lock. His blue eyes brightened. I could smell him grin.

"Wells," he said. He chuckled.

The door closed. I heard the scrape and rattle of the chain. The door opened. I walked across the threshold.

Kendrick kept on grinning at me, his yellow teeth showing, his white lips curled in. His head bobbed up and down. He chuckled some more. He always was a big chuckler.

He wasn't much over thirty. He hardly looked seventeen. He had that real smooth skin some pale people get. He wore soiled clamdiggers like a teenager, and flowered shirts. The expression he wore—an expression of stupid cunning —added to his youthful appearance. It made him look like a high-school kid peeking through the keyhole of the girls' locker room. He had a big sloping caveman's forehead. His blue eyes were sunk deep under it. Over it, straight, fine blonde hair flopped down onto his eyebrows. Now and then he had to swipe at it to get it out of his way.

"Mayforth." I nodded at him. He grinned and chuckled. He sniffled. He wiped his nose with his shirt sleeve.

"You're sweating," he said. "Wanna beer?"

"Yeah."

The kitchenette was behind a counter to my right. He went to it, opened the fridge. I looked around the little studio. It was cheap enough, but surprisingly neat. There was a tired orange rug over most of the floor. A frayed peach-colored sofa stood under the windows on the far wall. Flowered curtains hung above it. They barely stirred in the August air. There were orange director's chairs stationed here and there. Lots of colored pillows on the floor to sit on. A rickety writing table with a flower vase on top. Posters on the wall: harbors, dancers, grassy parks. The gentler impressionists.

Kendrick slouched over. He shoved a bottle of Bud into my hand. He grinned. He chuckled. He sniffed.

I tossed my coat over a director's chair. "Nice place."

"Thanks."

"Yours?"

"Nah. A friend's." His head bobbing, Kendrick moved toward the writing table.

I swigged the beer. "Delilah throw you out?"

He chuckled. "Nah. Well: yeah. You know."

"Sure. I know. You're pimping again. She warned you."

He wrestled with the table's drawer. The table shook on its spindly legs. The flower vase tilted, fell over. A little water puffed out the top.

"Shit," said Kendrick. He grabbed the vase as it rolled toward the edge. He straightened it with both hands. "Well, she's not exactly a corporation in herself, you know. I gotta expand." He managed to get the drawer open this time. Sweat dripped into it from his forehead. He paused to lift his shirt and wipe his face. I could see his ribs poking through the tight skin over his abdomen. He dropped the shirt. He sniffled, swiped at his nose with his sleeve.

I pulled my pack of cigarettes from my pocket. I shot one into my mouth, held my lighter to it. I watched him rooting in the drawer.

He was the scion of a noble clan, Mayforth was. His father, Mayforth Junior, was a big-time Broadway producer. Mayforth the Original, our man's gramps, had been one of those rare financial types who made a bundle during the Great Depression.

With Mayforth III, the bloodline had clearly peaked. Born and bred in some of the sniffier neighborhoods of Westchester, he was introduced early to the very cream of society. In youth, he mingled with the famous and the rich. He dined in all the glamor spots Manhattan has. Celebrities had him on their A list. Now and then, his gorgeous puss even graced the columns of the *Star* or the *News*.

At eighteen, like his father before him, he was packed off to Yale. He was supposed to join the dramatic society. Become a Whiffenpoof or whatever. He was supposed to learn the ins and outs of high-toned show business so he could follow in his father's footsteps.

Instead, he learned that if he put certain chemicals in his body, life turned into a merry game. He injected, he dropped, and he sniffed. He liked it. He liked to see the funny colors. He liked to watch with a lazy smile as they went by. In the generosity of his happy heart, he even liked to share his wonderful chemicals with others. For a small price. One day he offered this exchange to an undercover police officer who was responding to a dormitory complaint. His father kept him out of jail. The dean kicked him out of Yale. Then his father disowned him.

So that was maybe ten years ago. Since then, Mayforth had become a phantom on Theater Row. He haunted the cafés on Broadway and West Forty-second Street, down in the Village and Soho. Anywhere theater people went, there went Mayforth. He peddled his wares to his old dinner companions and to companions of his companions. Sometimes drugs, sometimes women, sometimes personal services, like running messages or paying off a cop.

The cops, of course, also used him. Now and again, they'd haul him into the back of a squad car, lean their grizzled faces into his, and paint unpleasant pictures of what life was like on Riker's Island. When they felt he had those pictures fixed firmly in his mind, they'd ask him questions about this drug supplier or that big-time customer. Now and again, they found him very helpful. And once, they passed him on to me.

I was writing a series on drugs in show business. A friend of mine on the force gave me Kendrick's name. He was nervous about talking to me at first. But I took him out to some good restaurants, treated him like a celebrity interview. After a while, he relaxed and gave me what I wanted. After a while longer, he began to have fun. He found he'd missed seeing his name in the papers. And even though his name had now become "unidentified source" it still gave him a kick. Since then, he'd called me every so often. Whenever he thought he had something that might interest me. Sometimes his price was a good dinner. Sometimes he took cash.

When he straightened at the writing desk now, he was holding a manila envelope. He wrestled the drawer shut. He stepped over—but hesitated before he handed the envelope to me.

"I mean, this is gonna cost you. You know? I mean, this is really money here. You know what I mean?"

I let my cigarette dangle between my lips and reached out with my free hand. He parted with the envelope. I sat down on the nearby director's chair. I set my beer on the floor. With smoke trailing up into my eyes, I pried the manila flap open.

Kendrick, meanwhile, plopped onto one of the floor pillows. There was a small cassette player next to him. I noticed now that it was spinning out a soft guitar melody. Next to the player was an ashtray. In the ashtray was a burnt-out reefer. Kendrick set the joint between his lips and lit it up again. He sucked in the drug with a noise like a busted steam pipe. He leaned back against the base of the sofa. He stared at me. He smiled dreamily.

There were photographs in the envelope. I paused to pluck the cigarette out of my mouth. I flicked an ash onto the carpet. I rubbed it with my shoe until it didn't show. I stuck the cig back into my face. I pinched the edge of the photographs and pulled them out.

Mayforth Kendrick III chuckled. His head bobbed up and down. He sucked his dope. He sniffled.

I examined the pictures, one at a time. Sweat ran off my temples, down my jaw. I smiled around my cigarette. I laughed. Kendrick chuckled.

"What is she, one of your girls?" I laughed again. "Oh shit, look at this."

Kendrick snorted. "Aren't they something?" He blew out a lungful of weed. "Nah. She's one of these actress types."

"Oh yeah," I said. "A model."

"Yeah. She might even be willing to talk."

"I'll bet. Jesus, look at this." I squinted at the pictures through the smoke. I shook my head. "Paul Abingdon. I'll be damned. What happened? Wouldn't he pay for these?"

"Hey." He pointed at himself with the fingers of both hands. "Let's just say I found it, uh, expedient, you know, to come to you. Okay? I mean, ask me no questions, know what I mean?"

"Yeah. Yeah, I think I know what you mean, Mayforth."

I slid the pictures back into the envelope. I tossed the envelope onto the carpet. I picked up my beer, pulled my cigarette free. I sat back in the director's chair and looked at my youthful friend. His head kept bobbing happily. He let out his laugh in a stuttered hiss: *chh chh chh.*

The smoke from my cigarette drifted lazily toward the open window. It mingled with the marijuana, with its acrid stench. The haze of smoke hung in the air. It hung there like the hot mist outside. Just sitting there, I felt damp all over. My palms sweat. There was sweat in the rings beneath my eyes.

"These are pretty raw," I told him. "I mean, I work for a family newspaper."

He spread his hands like he was giving a blessing. "Hell, you know, like, you X out the bad stuff. You can do that. I've seen them do that."

"Maybe. Maybe big X's."

"Anyway, man, those're just to, you know, convince you, see? There're the other ones in there, too, right? That one in the underwear. And where she's got his shirt on, you could crop that one. That one would look really nice." He shaped it for me in the hazy air. "Front page, you know."

"Uh-huh." I nodded. "Yeah. That's where they'd probably put it, all right. And just how much are you looking to earn here?"

He shrugged. "Whatever. You've always been fair to me, Wells. Truly." He whipped the limp blond hair back out of his eyes.

"The magazines might pay you more, you know. They would, for certain."

"Yeah, but . . . I mean, like . . . I *know* you, Wells." He chuckled loudly, and said again: "I *know* you."

I swigged more beer. My cigarette had burned to the filter. I slipped it through the neck of the Bud bottle. I heard the fire of it hiss and die.

I set the bottle down on the floor. I stood up. "I don't think so, pal."

Kendrick's jaw dropped. He jutted his face at me, eyes wide. "Man, did you see those? That's a congressman, man, a senate candidate."

"Thanks, Mayforth. I'm a newspaperman. I know who's running for senate." I picked my jacket off the chair. I tossed it over my shoulder.

Kendrick didn't leave his pillow. He didn't even stop suckling the drug. But he extended his hands at me between tokes. He implored me. "Come on, man. Did you see the one where he's got her tied up with his handkerchief? This is a married man we're talking about here."

"Yeah, yeah."

"He's hitting her with her, what is this, her sash or something. . . . You want a fucking SM freak in the United States Senate?"

"Why not? It's where all his friends are."

"Oh man!" He threw his hands up. They landed in his lap.

I smiled. "Sorry, Mayforth. They're good shots, they really are."

"I mean, I went to a lot of trouble, man," he said dejectedly.

"And don't think I don't appreciate it."

He hung his head. "Oh, man." I felt sorry for him.

"Lookit," I said. "The pictures are great. Really."

"You think it's easy with a fucking senate candidate?"

"Only you could have done it."

"Hey. I mean, no shit, you hear me?"

"The thing is," I said, "it's just not a story."

"What are you talking about?"

"It's no story, Mayforth. The guy's running for senate, not pope. His private life is nobody's business but his."

Mayforth Kendrick raised his eyes to heaven. "I can't believe this," he told the Lord. He lowered his eyes. "You know—somebody's gonna take them."

"Yeah," I said. "I know."

"I mean, stuff like this, man—it's in all the papers. It's juicy. It's scandal. It's good copy."

I shrugged. "So try the *Post*. Me, I think a candidate should screw as many people as he can. It's good practice in case he gets into office." I pulled the door open and stepped out. "See you later, Mayforth. Put in some air-conditioning."

"Oh man! I mean: man!" he was saying, as I closed his door and headed down the hall.

2

The heat hung on into morning. The sky stayed faint and bluish-gray. The air stayed heavy, full of rain that wouldn't fall. By 7:30, the temperature was eighty-five. There was no breeze.

I woke up sweating. I showered. I dried myself. I sweat. I put some clothes on over the sweat. I went out and had the Artful Dodge excavated from its garage. Usually, I take the subway to work. But the airless tunnels, the crowded cars, the smell of filth and piss could not entice me in this heat despite their charms. My ancient maroon Dart was air-conditioned, at least. At least, the vents hissed and coughed out a little stream of air.

I drove downtown on Lexington. Rush-hour busses jammed the way. They spewed black exhaust out behind them. The storefronts lining the dismal avenue shimmered under the stuff.

Otherwise, the traffic wasn't too bad. New York in August is a sleeping beast. The rich are gone to Europe, the almost rich are in their summer houses. The workers take their weeks off on the Jersey shore. Only the homeless stay. The sane ones in their shelters, the mad ones in the street. You see them—the mad ones—more and more as July wears on. As the well-fed fade away, they become more obvious. First, they're a face in a hundred, then in fifty. By the deeps of August, it seems they're one in ten. One in ten faces scum-blackened and slack-jawed. They sleep in doorways. They root through garbage. They mutter to themselves and shout to everyone else. They sit against the walls and stare. And the city goes quiet around them. Pretty soon, the mad are staring at each other. And at the reporters, I guess, who stay on too.

The reporters stare into the empty air. There's no news in August. Some fires if you're lucky. Some short-temper murders in the worst of the heat. Maybe a drought or a riot for a special treat. Other than that, nothing. The politicians aren't even pretending to work, and the civil servants don't see any point in striking. Even the top-notch bad guys take a breather. A crime-and-scandal man like me finds himself trying to remember what his byline looks like.

I'd been working on some good stuff as June ended. I'd finally gotten Robins indicted in Brooklyn for the payoff in Corlies Park. And I'd just hooked into a little police kickback deal that showed some promise of settling an old score between me and my good friend Lieutenant Tom Watts. But as June became July and July turned into August, the sources dried up. The flow of information slowed to a trickle. In this morning's edition, the only sign of the name John Wells was under the headline: SUSPECTED PUSHER WOUNDED IN CHASE. It was pathetic.

The buildings got taller and the traffic thicker as I hit midtown. Still, even on the sidewalks near Grand Central Terminal, the shirts-and-ties and jeans-and-T-shirts were not crushed together as usual. They moved fairly freely, though slowly, through the exhaust-laden heat. And in the spaces between them, I saw the mad and the homeless sitting against the walls. Their eyes followed me as I drove by.

I turned off Lex, tooled over to Vanderbilt Avenue. I parked in the press lane before the concrete tower that houses the *Star*.

I rode in an elevator with five other people. I could smell their deodorant and perfume turning sour with sweat.

A woman said, "When is it going to rain?"

A man said, "September."

I got out on twelve. I pushed through the glass doors into the *Star* city room. The blast of air-conditioned air washed over me. I sighed loudly.

The place was nearly empty. Almost no one moved in the vast maze of white walls that separated one cubicle from another. There wasn't even much activity at the city desk in the center of the room. Only the wires editor, Shelly Smith, was there, tapping at her computer. I glanced at my watch. It was quarter past nine. It seemed the city summer had brought the place to a halt.

I wandered over to the coffee machine against the wall. The coffeepot was empty.

I screamed: "Alex!"

My voice faded away into the hum of the electric clock on the wall above my head.

Seriously disgruntled, I carried the pot to the city desk. I lowered over Shelly, a pleasant-faced matron with frosted blond hair.

"Where the hell's the copy boy?" I said.

She did not look up. She tapped at her computer.

"Gone."

"What does that mean?"

"He got a job on the Philly *Inquirer*. Editor-in-chief, I think." She kept tapping.

"Didn't he make coffee before he left?"

"Maybe, but he left last Friday. It's probably cold."

"So who's the new copy boy?" I said.

"Fran."

"Fran!" I screamed.

A sylph with long black hair appeared. She wore a pleated purple skirt and a lavender blouse. She had a cute, round monkey-face with big square glasses perched on the little nose. I tossed the coffeepot into her arms. Startled, she caught it.

"Make some coffee fast," I said.

She did not move fast. She did not move at all. She hesitated. She looked at the coffeepot. She looked at me.

I pointed a finger at her. "Fran," I said, "I look into your young eyes and I see a girl debating whether to tell me that making coffee isn't part of her job."

"Well, I . . ."

"Make coffee, Fran."

"But when I was hired . . ."

"Fran. You don't understand. If you don't make coffee, I will rip your fucking head off and throw your bleeding carcass onto the street where the jackals can eat it."

Fran's mouth opened. Her cheeks flushed. She appealed to Shelly.

"He can do it," Shelly said. "It's in his contract."

Fran went away to make coffee.

"Black," I called after her. I sat on the edge of the city desk. "Imagine that Alex," I said. "He didn't even say good-bye."

"I know." Shelly pouted at her computer screen. She kept tapping the keys. "And after the way you treated him, too."

I lit a cigarette. "So that explains Alex. What about everyone else?"

"Everyone else is here."

"You're it? Is the whole staff on vacation?"

"The whole staff is at the whole staff meeting."

I paused in the midst of a breath of smoke. "Shit," I said.

"The nine A.M. staff meeting."

"Shit," I said again.

"And it's no good saying 'shit.' "

"Goddamn," I said.

"That's no good either. If I were you, I'd get going. Cambridge seemed put out by your absence."

"I forgot."

Shelly glanced up at me.

"Well, they slip my mind. It's Freudian."

She turned back to the monitor. "See a psychiatrist." She tapped away.

"I can't afford a psychiatrist. I'm about to get fired." I

got off the desk. "The guy doesn't even let us smoke," I muttered. "I'm forty-six. I should be able to smoke any-where I damn well please."

I wandered over toward the hall. I paused at the edge of it, smoking, trying to get as many drags in as I could.

Fran came to me with a Styrofoam cup full of black coffee. She handed it over.

"Thanks," I said. "Is my tie straight?"

"Your tie isn't even tied."

"Oh." I yanked it off, stuffed it in my jacket pocket.

"You're John Wells, right?" she asked.

"Yeah." I tried on a smile. "How's this? Does this look like I'm eating shit?"

Fran laughed. "No. It looks like you're chewing flesh."

"Darn."

"Alex told me about you," she said. She put her hands behind her back. She turned this way and that like a flirting schoolgirl.

"Yeah. Well, he was an idiot."

"He said you were the best reporter alive."

"A brilliant boy. He'll go far."

She lowered her eyes shyly. "He also said you were the biggest son of a bitch he'd ever met in his life."

"That Alex. What a kidder." I sipped my coffee. I tugged desperately at the last of my cigarette.

"And," added Fran, "he said if I called you 'Pops' you'd get really angry."

"Sage counsel, kid."

"So what I want to ask is: How will I know when you're really angry?"

I handed her the smoldering filter of my cigarette. "You won't," I told her. "But your survivors will."

I carried my coffee down the hall to the conference room.

The gang was all there. Editors, reporters, the lot. The elder statesmen, like Rafferty and Gershon and me, were a shaggy bunch with open vests and rolled-up sleeves and undone ties. The new breed, and they were in the majority now, were shiny and tidy and blow-dried. Old and young, they sat in chairs around the long conference table or stood behind the chairs with their backs against the wall. All of them looked up when I came in. The staff meeting has a thousand eyes.

Two of those eyes belonged to Robert Cambridge, our managing editor. He was one of the younger breed, thirty-three or so. He was sitting at the head of the table. He was slouching in his chair, his legs out before him. He looked sleek and trim in his tailored brown suit. He was playing with his pen. He was talking. Then he stopped talking. He looked up. He smiled at me. He smiled thinly.

"Johnny. Hey. Johnny," he said softly. "Have a seat."

He waved a hand at the chairs. All the chairs were taken.

"S'all right," I said. "I'll stand."

He nodded. "Great," he said, still softly. His voice was dangerously soft. "Great."

I moved to the back of the room. I excused myself as I pushed past the others in their chairs. Many of the editors studied the yellow legal pads in front of them as I went by. Many of my fellow reporters cleared their throats and murmured and stared at their laps. McKay, who was seated near the middle of the table, pinched the bridge of his nose with his fingers. His mouth wiggled back and forth.

I reached the back wall, leaned against it as the shifting and murmuring and staring continued another moment. I glanced down and was surprised to see Lansing seated right in front of me. She was supposed to be on vacation. She smiled up at me warmly. Her blue eyes softened. She reached out and touched my hand for a second.

"Hi, John! How are you? I missed you," she whispered.

I motioned her to face front. I figured I was in enough trouble. "Stop looking at me that way, Lansing," I hissed.

Her eyes clouded over on the instant. She was hurt. She turned away.

I sighed. I sipped my coffee. The morning was not going well. I peeked across the rim of my cup at Cambridge.

He did not look at me again. He looked at his pen. He
played with his pen, tapping it against the tabletop, letting
it slide up and down through his well-manicured fingers.
The expression on his round, tanned face seemed dreamy.
His voice oozed out. He seemed to just pick up where he'd
left off.

"Now, I've been here for almost—what has it been? Two
years," he said. "Two years . . . and certain things have
really changed and that's great. We've gotten much, much
more relatable as a newspaper. Much more oriented toward
what I always call Infotainment. Short pieces. People pieces.
You-and-me pieces. The kind of things people want to read.
We do much more of that now. And that's great."

The reporters nodded, staring down at the table. The
editors pretended to take notes on their legal pads. I sipped
my coffee, leaning against the wall.

Cambridge tapped his pen forcefully to punctuate his
words. "But we still . . . still—after all this time—we still
get bogged down in this—*idea*, this, this—*conception* of . . .
I don't know what you want to call it: The Holy Shrine of
News." The pen beat out the rhythm of his words. "I don't . . .
under . . . stand . . . why this . . . has . . . to be."

Next to him on the table lay a stack of newspapers. He
set the pencil down and grabbed one of them. He held the
paper up with one hand. It flopped forward, unreadable.
"The front page two weeks ago," he said. He jerked it to
get the page straight. It flopped forward. "Now why—" He
jerked it. It flopped. He straightened in his chair. He held
the paper in both hands, like Truman after he beat Dewey.
The banner read: DELLACROCE FREE. The crime boss, who'd
been sent up for racketeering barely a year before, had
been released after a technical appeal. I'd written the story.
"Now, I was out of town the week this happened," said
Cambridge, "and I come back and find this. And inside,
page eight or ten or I don't know what the hell it is, what
do we find out but that fucking Miss America may be married. I mean, fucking *married*, for Christ's sake!" He sur-

veyed our faces. We hung our heads in shame. "Page ten?"
he asked us. "I mean, okay, it turns out it wasn't true, but
I mean that's a *big* story! A big, big story! The *Post* led with
it and, okay, you can say what you want to about the *Post*
but they're not afraid to relate. To be relatable. Now that's
all I'm talking about."

He tossed the paper down, disgusted. He went on: What
foolish prejudice had caused us to lead with a freed mob
king when Miss America might be a Mrs.? he asked. Which
of those two stories were people more interested in? Which
were they more likely to talk about? Which would make
them stop and take notice, make them say to each other
over lunch, "Hey, did you see the *Star* today?"

"When you're doing a story, or assigning a story, or bud-
geting space for a story, ask yourselves those questions."
Cambridge said. "Ask yourselves: Is this just news, or is it
Infotainment?"

We listened. We shuffled our heels guiltily. We asked
ourselves the questions, just for practice. I asked myself:
Would our readers stop and take notice of Congressman
Paul Abingdon in the nude, lashing a naked woman with
her sash? Would they say to each other over lunch: "Hey,
did you see what was in the *Star* today? A senate candidate
with a hard-on!"

"I'm not pointing any fingers," Cambridge said in a mis-
chievous singsong voice, "but some people are just going
to have to get with the program here, okay? Because the
Star is going to be relatable. And that's the way it is, folks.
Okay?"

He must have felt this last part was a little rough on us.
He looked around at our dejection. He grinned his boyish,
lopsided, regular-guy grin. His forelock fell rakishly on his
forehead like a regular guy's. "So, hey," he said, raising his
eyebrows regular-guy-like. "Let's do it. What do you say?
Because this is good, good stuff we're doing here. It's important. Okay? Okay. Now . . ." He clapped his hands loudly.

"I ordered some Danish. Fran has put them out in the city room. Go out there. Enjoy it. It's on me. Okay?"

"Am I mistaken," murmured McKay, as we walked together back to the city room, "or is that man the biggest asshole who ever lived?"

"Oh, I don't know. What about Caligula?"

"No, no, no. He was a scumbag. That's different. I'm talking assholes."

I shrugged. McKay was our feature writer and resident wordsmith. He was always right when it came to questions of semantics.

In the newsroom, a crowd had now gathered around the coffee maker. There were two large boxes of doughnuts and Danish open there.

"Hey," said McKay. "It's on me. Okay?"

"Boy, you are just one regular guy."

"I know, I know."

"I'm talking regular."

We got ourselves some doughnuts and coffee. We carried them over to my cubicle. I plopped down in the chair. I shoved back a pile of newspapers. My Olympia was underneath, the last typewriter in the joint. I shoved that back too. I set down my breakfast. McKay, meanwhile, hoisted a pile of newspapers off the desk. He tossed them onto the floor. He sat down where the papers used to be.

"Didn't you get the memo on cleanliness?"

"Yeah, sure," I said. "I filed it next to godliness. It's in there somewhere." I chomped my doughnut. It was glazed. It was good. "So how's the kid?" I asked him.

McKay grinned, his face full of doughnut. He had a face like a kid himself. Round and all cheeks without a wrinkle on it. When he smiled, he looked like a diaper ad. "Oh great," he said. "She's starting to talk, it's really something. Yesterday, I come home . . ."

Lansing walked by, carrying a doughnut and coffee of her own.

"Yo," I called. "What brings you back so soon?"

She had been on some island or other, as I recalled. She was darkly tanned and her long blond hair had turned nearly platinum. She was wearing a white wraparound skirt and a yellow T-shirt. The skirt showed off her long bronzed legs. The shirt showed off the long, slim curves of her.

She didn't stop. I rolled my chair to the edge of the cubicle. I leaned my head out.

"Uh, Wells . . ." said McKay.

I didn't listen. "Yo, Lansing. Don't I get a hello?"

She stopped. She turned. Her skirt flared out as she turned. She walked slowly back to me. She smiled at me again. Weakly again.

Then she glanced down at the newspapers McKay had put on the floor.

"So how were the islands?"

"You know," she said tightly, "you don't have to do this." She pointed at the papers with her doughnut. "I mean, really, it only makes things worse."

I glanced at McKay. He was hiding his entire face in his coffee cup.

I tried again. "Yeah. So, uh, how were the islands?"

"I'm serious, Wells. I'm really serious."

I studied her face. A nice face to study. She had high cheekbones. She had white skin. She had rich lips, very red. But looking her over I realized she was right: she was serious.

"In that case," I told her, "it's McKay's fault."

McKay snorted some hot coffee through his nose. That, in turn, made me choke on my doughnut.

"It's not funny," said Lansing. I glanced at her again. Almost unbelievably, her eyes were damp. This is the woman who went into Washington House disguised as a drug addict last May. Came out with a series on halfway house abuse that shut the place down. "You know," she went on. Her lips thickened and trembled. "You come into the meeting half an hour late. You're not wearing a tie. You throw your papers out in the hall, and who do you think catches shit for it? Why do you think we have meetings like that?"

"Um—because Cambridge is an idiot?"

She made a swift, angry gesture with her doughnut. She dropped her voice. "All right. We know that. He's an idiot. But the people upstairs like him. And they have liked him for two years."

"They like everybody for two years," I said. "They liked Perelman when he came in to make us zingy, and Davis when he was going to give us pizzazz. Now, we're relatable. I've been here eleven years, Lancer. I've seen all the Cambridges come and go. . . ."

"Oh . . ." She spluttered a moment. Coffee slopped over the rim of her cup. It pattered onto the floor. "Big deal!" she hissed finally. "You and Rafferty, you sit together and plot and you got your big deal crime-boss story on the front page and you . . . you buried Miss America when he was out of town, giggling about it like a couple of children. And the younger people, you know, they respect you, you're a legend to them. You've backed him right to the wall, John. You've completely undermined his authority. You think he doesn't know who's responsible?"

"Uh—do I care?"

"You *should* care." She'd raised her voice. She looked around and lowered it. "You should care," she hissed. "Because he hates your guts. He hates your guts and he's gunning for you and the people upstairs love him and you should have a column by now and *you* could be secure and well-off instead of living in that dive and . . ."

"Lansing!" The cry came from the city desk. She looked around for it, her whole body trembling. "Lansing—your mother—on line four!"

Blood rushed into Lansing's high cheeks. She bared her teeth. "God *damn* it!" she said.

Her coffee sloshing, her doughnut dropping crumbs, she stormed off to her cubicle.

Open-mouthed, I swiveled to McKay. "Come out of that

coffee cup, you coward," I said. He surfaced, gasping. "What the hell was that?"

He thought it over. "Rage, I'd say. Maybe just anger . . . no. No, I'd have to say rage."

"Jesus Christ. She must have had a great vacation. I thought she wasn't due back until Monday, anyway."

McKay shrugged. "Maybe she didn't have a good time. She went with her mother."

"Is that my fault?"

McKay laughed. "I wouldn't answer that if it were the last question on earth. But I'll tell you this much: she's been snapping like a windup alligator all morning. She's had four cups of coffee. Her mother's called twice. . . . In fact, the only pleasant things she's said to anyone are 'How's Wells?' 'When's Wells coming in?' and 'Did Wells notice I was gone?' Hell, I thought she was gonna be nice to *you*."

"Yeah," I said. "She was." I lit a cigarette. "Christ, look at this. She's got me so upset, I lit a cigarette when I haven't even finished my doughnut yet."

McKay slid off my desk. "Hey," he said, as he left. "Enjoy it. It's on me. Okay?"

"Oh, shut up." He was gone. I shouted, "Fran!"

The sylph came running. Breathless: "What?"

"Clean up those goddamned newspapers," I said.

And that, it turned out, was the high point of my day. The rest was pure August. I read the paper. I finished my cigarette. I finished my doughnut, then another cigarette, then my coffee. Then I got on the phone. I dialed the cops on the killing of a trial witness in Brooklyn. They'd gotten nowhere. I smoked some cigarettes. I followed up a lead on a cable TV payoff. A dead end. I smoked. I called up the U.S. Attorney's office to flirt something out of one of his assistants. She was on vacation. I went down the hall to the room with the vending machine. I bought a new pack of butts. I returned. I sat. I smoked.

At one point, humbled, I even read the daybook. It was

some half-dozen items long and the most exciting one was a Mets pitcher visiting a children's hospital. I grabbed the phone again. I grabbed my cigarettes. I couldn't think of anyone to dial. I glanced at my watch. It was quarter to twelve. I dialed Siegel's deli and ordered a club sandwich. I figured it would be noon by the time it arrived. Late enough to take an hour off for lunch. I smoked, waiting for the sandwich.

McKay, meanwhile, was doing a feature on the swimming facilities at St. Bartholomew's. He came back around two P.M. His hair was damp. He was whistling. Around three, Lansing beat me to the door on a scaffold collapse. It didn't turn out to be much. Only four people were injured. I felt bad for trying to trip her as she ran past.

Deadline approached for the bulldog. I smoked and tried to think of people to call. Rafferty, who is the city editor, emerged from the budget meeting. He walked over to my cubicle. He told me they were going national with the front page. He is a bullet-headed old cuss with a shell of imperturbable calm. He never raises his voice above a tight-lipped murmur. But I sensed an accusation in his tone.

I smoked. The city offices were closed now. Only the cops were left, and you could only reach them at P.I.O. They had just heard about the scaffold collapse. We had more on it than they did. They did have a drug killing in the Heights, but it had cleared the wires half an hour before. They had nothing new to add. I asked Rafferty if he wanted me to rewrite the wire copy. "Don't, John. Don't debase yourself," he said. I went back to my cubicle.

The deadline came. The deadline went. No story by John Wells. I smoked. The next edition's deadline came and it went too and still no story. By the deadline for the final edition I had given up. I sat at my desk staring at the pile of papers with my typewriter under it. I smoked the last of my second pack of cigarettes. I cursed the gods of summertime.

I looked around me. The day was gone. Lansing and

McKay had left. The lanes between the cubicles were as quiet as when I had come in. Only Rafferty remained and he practically lived here. Even he was now handing the reins over to Wendy Miller, the night city editor.

I finished my cigarette. I was all out. I stood up, cursing. I grabbed my coat off the back of my chair. I tossed it over my arm. I walked through the maze to the city desk.

Rafferty was thumbing through some hard copy. Miller was looking over his shoulder. It was very quiet. Only the police scanners blurped and fizzled.

Rafferty did not look up at me. "Another wasted day, I see," he murmured.

"No news is good news, Rafferty. Just think of me as the bearer of good news."

"Now, now." He barely moved his lips. "You're just not trying. Remember: relatability."

"Relatability."

"Keep saying it."

"Good night, Rafferty."

" 'Night, deadweight."

I tossed my coat over my shoulder. "Relatability," I repeated to myself. I wandered to the glass doors. I pushed one open. The muggy heat stormed over me.

"Hey, Wells," Rafferty mumbled.

I leaned my back against the open door, looked at him. He had reached for the scanner. He was fiddling with the squelch dial.

"Mayforth Kendrick III," said the city editor. "He's one of your buddies, right?"

"Yeah, he's my twin brother, why?"

Rafferty cocked his head, listening. Nothing came from the little box but static.

"I just heard a call about him."

"Sound like they're gonna bust him?" I asked.

"Sounds like they're gonna bury him," said Rafferty. "Sounds like he's dead."

3

The short, scummy life of Mayforth Kendrick III had been extinguished by a .22 caliber slug. It had drilled a neat little rust-colored hole in the center of that Cro-Magnon forehead of his. Then it had continued right on through his skull into the softer stuff of his brain. It had turned off the lights in there just as easy as flicking a switch.

That's what he looked like, lying there. Like someone had turned him off right in the middle of things. He lay on his back at the center of the orange rug. Just in front of the director's chair I'd been sitting in the night before. He had his arms thrown out on either side of him. His eyes were still open. His mouth was still shaping the scream it had meant to make before the lights went out.

I turned away from him. I left him to the crowd of forensic types crouched by his body. I walked back to Fred Gottlieb. He shook his head at me as I came.

"Are you hot?" he said. "I'm hot today."

He was leaning against the kitchenette counter. He looked hot. His white jacket seemed to hang heavy on him. There were beads of sweat caught in the black swatches of hair that poured out of his open peach shirt. The shirt's middle, stretched tight by his big belly, was dark and damp. The sweat shone on his high forehead. It dribbled from what was left of his curly black hair. It creased his round, rough, swarthy face. He kept his lips parted slightly, as if he was panting.

I leaned against the counter next to him. "Everybody's

hot," I said. I looked down at the backs of the men crouching over poor Mayforth. All around them, other men and women scurried. Men mostly, mostly in their forties. Most of them were wearing gray suits. Most of them had bare pates that shone with sweat. Some had briefcases, some had cameras. Some were leaning over, painting furniture with fingerprint dust. Some were crawling along the carpet on their hands and knees, plucking out prizes and dropping them in plastic bags. Some were opening drawers and cabinets, going through the contents.

"No, really," said Gottlieb. "I feel especially hot. Maybe I have a fever, I don't know, I could be walking around with a hundred and four, I'll catch pneumonia." He wiped his face with the palm of his hand.

"I wouldn't worry, Fred."

"Of course not, why should you worry? Do you have a fever? No."

"Fred, it's ninety-five degrees at ten o'clock at night. It's hot. You're hot because it's hot. We're all hot."

"Eesh. I don't know. Maybe that's it." He felt with his fingers for the pulse at the base of his neck. "You think that could be it?"

A flash snapped. It seemed to add to the thick night heat. Two men brought a stretcher to the door. One of the forensic guys, McFadden I think his name was, stood up from Mayforth's body. He wiped his brow with his sleeve. He saluted to Gottlieb and backed away. Gottlieb made a gesture to the attendants at the door. Someone moved a chair out of the way. The attendants carried in the stretcher and laid it next to the corpse.

Gottlieb shook his head again. "Such a thing," he said. "It's a terrible, terrible thing."

"Yeah. Poor little weasel," I said.

"A terrible thing," he repeated. "It could happen to anyone—just like that, you wouldn't even know why."

"Oh, I don't know," I said. "With a guy like Kendrick, there's usually a pretty good reason."

"It's a blessing his father isn't alive to see this, he would be ashamed, and who could blame him, his own son." Gottlieb rubbed at the sweat on his chest hairs. He examined his wet palm. "Eesh," he said. He glanced at me sideways. "And? So? Why're you out so late burying weasels?"

I snorted. "It's slow. Anyway, there's the Broadway connection. Anyway, I knew him."

"I forgot. That's right."

"What about you? I thought lieutenants only did presidents and popes and, like, locked-room mysteries."

The small brown pools of Gottlieb's eyes glittered. "I should be so lucky. I work. He's shot. I'm here."

The two attendants had unrolled a body bag now. They fitted Kendrick in it gently. Feet first, then pulling it up. Lifting him to get it on, as if he were a baby being changed. Then they pulled it over his head and zipped it up. Kendrick's face disappeared behind the plastic. The shape of his nose and forehead could be traced in the bag. I caught myself wondering how he'd be able to breathe like that.

I watched as the attendants lifted the body bag onto the stretcher.

"So what's the word, Fred? What have you got?"

The burly detective groaned. "You could get cholera in this heat. I've heard of that. Places like Africa. They get cholera from the heat."

"I thought that was from the water."

"The water, the heat," he said. "It's the heat on the water that makes it like that. Look at this." He turned a bit away from me. "Is there a rash here on the back of my neck?"

"No, no, you're fine. Anyway, it's from shit."

"The rash."

"No, cholera." The bag holding the corpse of Mayforth Kendrick III was carried out the door. "I remember now. They get it from drinking water with shit in it."

"Eesh, that's disgusting," Gottlieb said, screwing up his face. "Why do they do that?"

"I don't know. I guess it's a ritual or something."

Above the voices of the investigators around the room, I could hear the banging of the stretcher men on the stairs. I heard them mutter instructions at each other. I heard their voices fading. Then they were gone. A few moments later, the siren of the ambulance began. Then that faded away too.

"Well," said Gottlieb. "It can't be good for you, this heat."

"You'll live."

He put his hand on his stomach. "Eesh," he said again.

McFadden, or whoever he was, wandered over. He was a short, thin man. His suit was light gray. So was his hair, what there was of it. He pressed his fists into his kidneys and stretched backward, grunting.

"So?" Gottlieb asked him.

McFadden shrugged with his eyebrows. "Shot dead with a twenty-two."

"When?"

"When'd you get the call about the gunshot?"

"I don't know. Half hour, forty-five minutes."

"I'd guess it happened half hour, forty-five minutes ago," said McFadden.

"For this your mother sent you to medical school?"

McFadden broke his stretch with a laugh. "I'll call you after the autopsy. We'll do lunch."

"Thanks. After an autopsy, I do seltzer. I do Pepto."

McFadden waved and walked to the door.

"After the autopsy . . ." Gottlieb muttered. He pushed off the counter. He was ready to go to work. Around the room, the eyes of half a dozen investigators shifted toward him.

"Listen," I said, "I've got something."

He paused. He rubbed the back of his neck again. He looked annoyed with it. "So?"

"So let's play."

He gave a big shrug. "Fine. We'll play, we'll talk, we'll know things together."

"Terrific. You first."

"Me first. I just got here. What could I know?" Now his head went from side to side. "Kendrick—you knew him— Kendrick was a *shmendrik*. He hung around with other *shmendriks*. One of these alleged *shmendriks* had a gun. A bad situation: a *shmendrik* with a gun. And Mayforth is a fond memory for all of us." Another big shrug. "What else? We're searching the area. We're browbeating the land- lord . . ."

"How come?"

"He didn't live here. Kendrick. You know that. He lived with Delilah Rose formerly Shasta Jones formerly a not- very-high-priced lady of the evening. The landlord, a not- very-reputable fellow named Ray Leonard, he tells me this apartment was rented by a woman who called herself April Something . . . Thomas . . . formerly somebody else prob- ably . . . He says she paid in cash monthly with no lease —Mr. Leonard never heard of the housing code—and he doesn't know anything else about her. So what I want to know is: who's April Thomas and why is Mayforth Kendrick in her apartment?"

"She's probably one of his new girls. He told me he was pimping again. That's why Delilah eighty-sixed him."

"This explains many things. One puts him out, one takes him in. Somebody else takes him out." Gottlieb heaved a big sigh. "What a life. Was he pimping this neighborhood?"

"That I don't know."

"It would explain many another conundrum."

"This someone's neighborhood already?"

"I would say, yes. Alphonse Marino, he would also say yes."

"Oh Christ. Mean man, Alphonse. I thought he strong- armed for Dellacroce."

"He does this on the side. He's an entrepreneur," Gott- lieb said.

"Poor Kendrick."

"Poor Kendrick."

"So what. You gonna look for the girl?"

"The girl, a gun, a clue, a tip. We'll take an anonymous tip. Anything. Now," he said. He focused those oddly gentle little eyes on me. "I played. So you play."

"Can I smoke in here?"

"Oh, God, don't, it's so bad for you. Eesh. Cancer. It's a disaster. You don't want to know about it. Anyway, this is a crime scene. It's not allowed."

"Thanks." I lit a cigarette. It tasted sharp in the heat. I took a long drag all the same.

"Use the ashtray on the counter," Gottlieb said. "It's been dusted already." He kept watching me. He wiped his neck. He shook his jacket to air out his underarms. He mopped his face with a handkerchief. But his eyes stayed on me.

I took another long drag. I stalled.

"Hello?" said Gottlieb.

"Yeah, yeah." There was nothing for it. Even if I could get away with withholding evidence as a reporter, I couldn't do it to Gottlieb. He was a friend, not to mention my best contact on the force. "Okay," I said. I sighed smoke at him. "Have you found any pictures?"

"Pictures?"

"Yeah, an envelope with pictures in it. It was in that table." I pointed at the table with the spindly legs.

Gottlieb looked over his shoulder at it. "We did that table. No envelope, no pictures. Which pictures are these?"

I took another drag. I let it out with another sigh. "Oh, you'd know these pictures," I said. "They feature one Congressman Paul Abingdon in frolicsome mood with one very naked blonde."

Gottlieb stared at me. His tongue was in his cheek. He chewed on it for a long time. "You saw these."

"Kendrick tried to sell them to me. Apparently he tried to blackmail Abingdon first, but when Paul wouldn't go, he tried me."

"When was this exactly?"

"Last night."

"You saw the dear departed last night? Did he look afraid

or anything? Did he say to you: make sure you shut the door when you come in, Wells, someone named such-and-such is coming over to kill me."

"Sorry."

Gottlieb sighed. "Just a thought. He was healthy, happy? Life was a song?"

"Yeah. He was just a little put out when I didn't take the pictures, that's all."

"You turned them down."

Now I sighed. I shook my head. "Guilty."

"You don't like selling newspapers?"

"I like selling newspapers with news."

"So?" Gottlieb looked around the busy room with a bemused expression. "Now it's news," he said.

"Yeah, I know it. Boy, do I know it." I followed his gaze around the room. I saw myself sitting there again. I heard myself telling Kendrick, *The thing is, it's just not a story.* I remembered the confidence in my voice when I said it. Now I said: "So does this make me a schlemiel or a shlimazl?"

Gottlieb chuckled. He reached out and patted my cheek with one hairy hand. It forced smoke out of my mouth. "It makes you a *mensch*," he said. "You should be in a decent profession without bodies in it. You should be a married person. Where's Lansing these days? I haven't seen her."

"Vacation. With the other kindergarten kids. Listen. Any possibility you can keep this picture thing under wraps? For a day or so?"

"Eesh," said Gottlieb.

"I know, I know. But eventually my boss is gonna find out I turned these pictures down. It's not gonna be pretty. And then if I get scooped on it, I won't have to worry about the decency of my profession."

Gottlieb waggled his head a little. Then he said, "Ooh!" and rubbed the back of his neck again.

"A rash on the back of the neck," he said. "What's that a symptom of?"

"The heat."

"No, really. Don't hide it from me, because you have to get these things right away, catch them early."

"It's heat rash, buddy, everybody gets it."

"This heat. I'm telling you: It's not a good thing."

"What do you think? About the pictures, I mean."

Now, the activity around the room seemed to be slowing down. Uniformed officers and plainclothesmen alike seemed to have come to rest at their stations around the room. They were waiting for Gottlieb. He glanced over his shoulder at them, held up his hand.

"I'll do what I can, my friend. But I can't exactly keep it from my own people. And this is New York. The press has more sources on the force than I have." He spread his arms helplessly. "I'll try."

"Thanks, pal." I crushed out my cigarette in the dusted ashtray. I headed for the door. "Remember: I can't support Lansing without a job."

"She won't wait forever, Wells," he called after me.

I laughed. "She's a kid."

He waved me off. "What do you know?" he said.

His people rallied round him as he moved to the center of the room. He stood before them mopping the back of his neck with the handkerchief. He was examining the sweat on the handkerchief with a look of deep concern when I went out the door.

4

My radio alarm went off at seven A.M.:

"The top story this hour: anonymous police sources are saying this morning that photos of Congressman Paul Abingdon may have played a role in last night's murder of a suspected drug dealer. The source described the photos of the senate candidate as being (quote) 'of a sexual nature.' According to the source, the murder victim, Mayforth Kendrick III, may have tried to blackmail the married Abingdon with the photos, and then tried to sell them to a reporter for the *New York Star*. Abingdon has been unavailable for comment so far. . . ."

My phone went off at seven oh one. I fumbled for it. Brought the handset to my ear.

"It had to be yooooou," someone was singing. "It had to be yooooou. . . ."

Himmelmann from the *Times*. I hung up on him. I rolled out of bed. I sat in my underwear on the edge of the mattress, my feet on the floor, my face in my hands.

At seven oh two, the phone rang again.

"Hi, John, this is Hank Larson at Channel Four. I was wondering. . . ."

"Hank, I'd like to talk to you, but I've gotta leave this line open. My managing editor is trying to reach me. Try me at the office in an hour or so. . . ."

I hung up on him too.

It was now seven oh three. The phone was ringing. I

cursed Alexander Graham Bell. I cursed Don Ameche. I picked up the phone.

"John." It was Cambridge. "John. John. John."

"Hey, Bob," I said. "Listen, I'd love to talk to you, but I promised I'd get in touch with Hank Larson over at Channel Four. . . ."

There was dead silence. I fumbled for the cigarettes on my nightstand. I lit one. No coffin nail ever tasted so good. Cambridge said: "John." He did not sound happy. He took a deep breath. I took a deep breath. "We have got a real problem here," he said. "A real problem."

In the next several seconds, I ran through every dodge I knew. At one point or another in my long, illustrious career, I have tried them all. I have avoided editors with feigned sicknesses and rigged cars. I've ducked their assignments by telling them the line was busy or the address was wrong. I even hid under a desk once to get out of calling some train wreck victim's widow. If there's any kind of daylight between an editor's stupid and misguided notion and my own crystal principles and lucid vision, I've snuck through it. But today, I felt I'd come to the end of my rope.

Eventually, one way or another, the fact that I was the reporter who turned down Kendrick's pictures was going to become common knowledge. I was guilty as sin of failing to be relatable, and sooner or later, the whole world was going to find out. I smoked my cigarette, grateful for small favors, and waited for Cambridge to go on.

Cambridge noticed my silence. He knew it for the capitulation it was. I guess he figured there was no point toying with me. He brought out his big guns.

"The people upstairs want to see you. They've asked me to arrange a meeting in the upstairs conference room for eight-thirty."

I glanced at the clock. It was seven oh five. It had been a long day.

"I'll be there," I said.

There was another silence. Then Cambridge said: "John."

Then he said: "John, John, John." Then he sighed. Then he hung up.

I placed the handset back in the cradle. The phone rang. I pulled the plug. I could hear the phone in the other room ringing. I waited. I sat on the bed. I smoked my cigarette. Finally, it stopped.

I threw on a bathrobe and wandered into the living room. I put the coffee on in the kitchen. The phone on the desk by the window started ringing again. I pulled the plug on that one, too.

I drank my coffee standing by the window. I peered out over the coffee's steaming surface. I looked down on Eighty-fifth Street. I watched the marquee of the triplex theater four stories below. Its lights were off. It seemed oddly pale and anemic in the early morning light.

Everything out there seemed that way. Pale, faded, quiet. It was the heat. The heat again. My air-conditioning was on, but I could feel it. The windows were closed and the smells and sounds and weathers of the street were muted. But I could feel it out there all the same. The heat. I could practically see it. The sun and the morning sky were covered by that faint, damp mist that had hung there for days. The sun burned white through it and washed out the city's colors with blank, unrelenting fire. The sun baked the sidewalk. There were few people walking there. Those who were walked slowly, bent over. The sun drained the color from the green newsstand and the black pavement and the white garbage trucks just starting to grind from station to station. The sun shone hot against my windowpane. I drank my coffee and I felt it and I sweat. The collar of my bathrobe grew damp and warm.

It was seven-twenty when I set the empty cup down on the table. I went into the bathroom. Showered, shaved and dressed. Now it was close to eight. I'd put on my best suit, a gray pinstripe. I'd put on a red-striped tie. Solemn but not somber. Introspective but not necessarily penitent. I gave myself the once-over in the mirror. I practiced rubbing my chin thoughtfully. I said, "Well, sir, you may be right," once or twice, trying to make it sound sincere.

It didn't sound very sincere.

It was eight o'clock. The man on the radio told me. Then he told me about Paul Abingdon again. He told me about the pictures of a sexual nature. Then he told me about the reporter for the *New York Star*. The reporter who was now believed to be John Wells.

"Shut up," I said. I killed the radio. I killed the air-conditioning. I killed the lights. I plugged in the phone. It started ringing. I killed the phone. I turned my back on it and walked away.

I went to the door and opened it. The heat hit me in the face like a fist.

Then a fist hit me in the face like the heat. It was a fist the size of a basketball. A black pit opened in my head. I stumbled backward and fell into it.

5

I was going to be late for my crucifixion.

That was the first thought that occurred to me as I opened my eyes. I was on the floor. I was on my back. I was looking up at the ceiling. I noticed the plaster up there was webbed with cracks. I noticed there were lights dancing up there like fairies. I noticed that the ceiling swayed: someone had forgotten to nail it down.

A shadow passed between me and these visions. The ceiling was blotted out. Oddly, the little dancing lights kept dancing even in the shadows. But then the fairies can do anything they want, can't they?

I squinted. I shook my head. The shadow began to resolve itself into a shape. Or several shapes. A human shape. Or the shape of several humans. I pushed up on my elbows. I squinted. The shapes of the shadow whirled sickeningly. Slowly, then, they joined together into one shape. One human. One enormous human. For a moment, as I tried to bring him into focus, he seemed to be bearing the ceiling on his shoulders.

The giant human shape spoke to me. It said: "God will punish you for what you have done."

"More?" I said. The word did not quite make it out intact. I worked my way into a sitting position. I groaned with the effort. I looked down between my knees. The floor was spinning.

"Beg for forgiveness," the giant shape above me said.

"Please forgive me," I muttered.

"Not from me, from God."

"Whoever hit me."

The shape lapsed into silence. The spinning of the floor was making my stomach spin, too. I shook my head to make it all stop. A barbell rolled across the floor of my brain.

Now, the shape crouched down in front of me. He really was huge. His head alone filled up my blurring vision. It was a round head with shaggy blond hair framing the face of it.

"God forgive me," he said in a soft, deep voice. "I . . . I shouldn't have turned to violence."

"I'll say."

"Let me help you."

He wrapped an enormous hand around my entire upper arm. He hoisted me to my feet. I was beginning to see more clearly. I could see he was a young man, maybe in his early twenties. Round-cheeked like a kid, with a sweet, open expression. With blue eyes that were troubled but clean and clear. On either side of that face, shoulders seemed to extend forever. From the shoulders, arms hung down thick and heavy as beef.

I nodded as he set me aright. The giant boy smiled shyly.

"Thanks," I said, and I kneed him in the balls.

He bent forward. I reared back and hit him in the face with the longest roundhouse I could throw. The force of the blow brought me spinning to the floor again. The giant, on the other hand, swayed back and forth for a long moment before he went down. He landed on his ass. I was on my hands and knees. He groaned. I gagged. I pushed my way back to my feet.

The giant was sitting propped against an easy chair. His nose was bleeding from the right nostril. His mouth hung open. His eyes gazed blankly into space.

I stumbled over to him and grabbed him by the shirt front. I tried to haul him up. It was like trying to haul a bag of sand. I tried again. I felt a sharp pain across my lower back. I grunted. I straightened. I stopped trying to lift him.

"Awrigh'," I said. "Wha the fubus dubus?" Somehow, that didn't sound right. I rubbed my hand over my forehead. It didn't seem to help. My legs seemed to be getting weaker by the second. I didn't think they would support me much longer. I staggered away from the sitting giant. I put my hands out in front of me. I reached for the swivel chair by the desk near the window. When I got hold of its arms, I pulled it to me. Gingerly, I lowered myself into it. I sat silently a moment, staring at the giant who sat silently staring into space.

"Shit," I said.

The giant turned his head toward me. He kept staring.

"Huh?" he said.

"Yeah," I said.

The giant raised one heavy hand to his face. He took it away. He stared at his palm.

"Blood," he said. "Blood. You hit me."

I nodded. "Thash righ'. And if I ever stand up, I'll do it again."

"Oh sweet Jesus, am I all right, am I alive?"

"How the hell should I know? What is this anyway?"

Now, the kid put both hands to his forehead. He let out a long moan. But it seemed more a sound of anguish than of pain.

"Oh, Father in Heaven, what have I done?"

"I'm not sure," I said. "But next time, knock on the door like anyone else."

"Huh?"

Then this thought seemed to get through to him. He nodded. He reached back and grabbed hold of the easy chair. He lifted himself into it. He felt the effort in his groin. He laid a hand on it and bent forward in the chair.

"Goshagorry," he said. "You really hurt me, Mr. Wells."

The quaking in my brain seemed to be slowing. When I spoke next, I could almost understand what I said. "At least you had the right man. Do I know you?"

"I don't think so. I'm Wally Shakespeare."

"Nope."

"But you know her, don't you?" Moving by painful inches, he dug into his pants pocket. He brought out a hefty black wallet. He opened it and held it out toward me.

I took it, looked it over. It was opened to a plastic folder. Through the fog and scratches on the surface of it, I could make out a picture of a girl. I caught my breath at the sight of her.

"Don't you?" said Wally Shakespeare.

I nodded. I handed the wallet back to him. "She looks good with her clothes on too," I said. It was the girl who had been with Abingdon in Kendrick's pictures.

The gargantuan kid rocketed out of his seat. I didn't think I'd left that much energy in him. Suddenly, he was towering over me again. His round face was scarlet. His fists were clenched at his sides.

"Shut up!" he said. "Shut up about her, that's all!" Then he brought his hands to his forehead. The fingers were curled up like claws. He cried out, "Oh God, help thy servant in his pain."

I decided he wasn't going to hit me again. I let out my breath. "Why don't you sit down, son? Start at the beginning." He nodded. He stumbled backward blindly. He dropped into the chair. He replaced his head in his hands.

The air conditioning had only been off a few moments, but already the heat was seeping in again. The air had begun to cling to me. It was like sitting in a swamp. It made my throbbing head throb more. I managed to get to my feet. I went into the bedroom and clicked on the a/c. As I passed, I glanced at the disconnected phone. I imagined Cambridge dialing on the other end. Dialing and dialing. Angrier and angrier. I glanced at my watch. It was eight twenty. A long, long day.

When I returned to the living room, Shakespeare was sitting just the way I'd left him.

"Have you got those sinful photographs?" he said miser-

ably. "Are you gonna put them in the newspapers for all
the world to see?"

"No. Hell no." I walked into the kitchen. I poured what
was left in the coffeepot into a pan. I put the pan on the
stove and turned the fire on under it. "You want coffee?"

"Huh? Yeah. But they said on the radio . . ."

"They said Kendrick tried to sell me the photographs."

"Yeah, that's right."

"They didn't say I bought them." I leaned in the kitchen
doorway. I lit a cigarette. "Say, you're not a reporter, are
you?"

He'd raised his head now. He looked at me blankly.
"Huh?"

"A joke. Never mind." He didn't seem to get it, but he
nodded anyway. "So what is this?" I said. "I take it you
know this girl."

He sniffled. He wiped away the blood from his nose with
the back of his wrist. He jerked his chin up and down, his
face forlorn. "She's my fiancé—" Fi-ansee, he pronounced
it. "She's my fiancée, Georgia Stuart."

The coffee bubbled in the pan. I poured a mug for each
of us. I brought him his. He set it on a lamp stand and
never touched it again. I brought mine to the desk and set
it there and never touched it again. I sat down in the desk
chair.

"All right," I said. "Hit me." He glanced up quickly. "A
figure of speech. Tell me everything."

"Oh." He sat forward in the chair, his hands dangling
down between his knees. He took a moment to gather his
thoughts. "You ever been to Ohio?" he asked.

"Passed through, yeah."

He laughed ruefully. "Golly, I wish I were there now.
Fallonville. You know it?"

I shook my head. Killed one cigarette, lit another.

"It's pretty," said Wally Shakespeare quietly. He smiled
at the opposite wall, like he could see it there. "Right around

this time. Hot, real hot, but not hot like this, you know? Not all wet and dirty like this, just . . . I don't know. Clean hot. Like it's supposed to be. Sky all blue. Fields kind of tan brown. And every now and then, a breeze sort of comes out of the high grass to cool you off, or you can go down to Fallon Creek and jump in off the rope. . . . You know what I mean?" He glanced over at me. I glanced at my watch. I'm gonna lose my job, and the Ohio tourist board is doing a presentation. Eventually, friend Wally went on. "Anyway . . ." He sighed for his lost state. "Anyway, it's just a small town, a little farming town, Fallonville. Fifteen thousand souls, maybe. If that. My dad's the preacher there. Only one. Does just about all the marrying and burying folks could ask for." He smiled fondly. "My dad . . ." he said. "His people were from over in Tankersville. They . . ."

"Son . . . Wally . . . Please," I said.

"Huh? Oh. You got an appointment or something?"

"Sort of. Yeah."

"Sorry. I forgot. This town: everybody rushing everywhere. No time for talking."

"It's a shame, I know. Now just lay it out for me, willya?"

"Right, right. It's just I haven't been back home in— golly, in six months now almost. I kind of miss it."

"Is that when you and Georgia Stuart got engaged?"

He nodded and looked away. He seemed to have to brace himself to go on. I watched the tip of my cigarette burning, the second hand of my watch moving. "I was down . . . See, I'm in school now myself over in High Corner, studying to be a preacher like my dad. It was at the end of the Easter holidays, though, and I was at home. So now, I noticed, while I was gone, a new shopping mall had opened up just a few miles down the highway, and my daddy, he was telling me how it was snaring young people and leading them into the ways of sloth and sin."

"Yeah," I said. "I've heard of those."

"You bet. You bet," he said. "So now my daddy, he figured whereas I was closer to these misguided young people by way of age, I might be more effective in preaching the gospel to them than he was. Because, see, he'd tried it. . . . He'd actually gone right down there, right into the lion's den itself and he'd preached to them, and they just laughed at him outright. I mean, this is the shepherd of God we're talking about, and they just laughed at him. So he said to me, 'Son, God has set before you a trial.' And I spent that night, Mr. Wells, I spent it watching and praying by my bed for guidance. And in the morning, I went down into the lion's den myself."

I looked at my watch. It was eight forty-five. I crushed out my cigarette. I lit another. The smoke hung in the still, thin, air-conditioned air.

"Well, armed with the gospel, I went down there," Wally Shakespeare said. He hunched his giant shoulders at the memory of his own heroism. "I walked right into the lion's den. Well, actually, it was the Burger King, but you know what I'm saying. And I addressed the poor sinning young folk gathered there in sloth and ignorance, gathered there in their torn denim jackets and their tight black jeans and their godforsaken haircuts and I said—" And his voice all at once became a deep, rolling earthquake of a thing—"I said, 'Verily, verily, I say unto you, unless you are born again, you cannot enter the Kingdom of God.'" He quieted down again. "Well, Mr. Wells, sir, those children gathered before me in the Burger King, they treated me just as they treated my father before me. Just as they've treated the prophets throughout the history of creation. Just like Isaiah and Jeremiah and Elijah himself, I was pelted with french fries and with the empty cups of milkshakes until I turned my head sadly and walked out into the parking lot."

I nodded sympathetically. It was a little tough to imagine Isaiah getting slapped with a side of fries, but I let it pass in the interest of time.

Wally said, "But I did not let the word of God fall silent. No, sir. I returned to that place the next day and the day after that, and I preached the gospel to those poor children again. And finally, praise be to God, one of them came forward." He paused. He had the timing of a preacher already. "And that was Georgia," he intoned. "She came to me, praise God, as I knelt out in back of the gas station asking the Lord to help me in my attempt to serve Him. And she said to me, I'll never forget it, she said, 'All right. I don't know much about this God stuff. But maybe—maybe you can show me the way.' "

He raised his head and stared into the middle distance. His blue eyes were alight with the memory and magic of it. I glanced at my watch. It was almost nine. I thought of lions' dens. My head hurt. "Yeah?" I said.

"I wish I could tell you what her face looked like in that moment, Mr. Wells," Wally said. "All fiery and blushing and full of the spirit. Her lips like cherries, and her eyes . . ."

"Right, like emeralds, yeah."

"No, like lapis."

"Wally, what happened next?"

His chin fell a little. But he pushed ahead. "For two days, Mr. Wells, I preached the gospel to her. We sat together side by side in my daddy's church and I read her scripture, page after page. And on the third day, Mr. Wells . . . On the third day, she reached out and she touched me on the leg, and I knew, I knew it was time for her to be baptised." His chin was inflating again. He was transported by the sweetness of the memory. "In the first light of that cool spring morning with the breezes blowing down from Apple Hill, she came to me at Fallon's Creek. You shoulda seen her. What she'd been like before—what she was like now. That's the glory of it, Mr. Wells, what it does for *people*, what it did for her. She was . . . all different. All . . . all tender and . . . and good again. Not dressed like some kinda hoodlum or something but, like, like a woman oughta dress with all . . . flowers on her dress and one of those . . . straw hats, you know, with ribbons on it. There's a picture of my mama, God rest her soul, on my daddy's bedtable, looks just like that . . . all good, Mr. Wells and . . . Good."

He lowered his eyes. Shook his head sadly at what he'd lost. It was another second before he drew in a sigh and continued. "We stood together in Fallon's Pond and I took hold of her. And I delivered her to the Lord and then . . ." And now he looked up at me with eyes that were far, far away. "Then . . . we became engaged."

I gave him a brief moment of silence. "So how'd she wind up in bed with Paul Abingdon?" I asked then.

His face turned scarlet. But this time, he did not seem angry at me. He glared bitterly at the cigarette burns in the floor. "The devil saw my prize," he said, his country-boy face twisted into a sneer. "The devil saw my prize and came in the jealousy of his evil heart and claimed her for his own. Mr. Wells, after that day, I never saw her again. I would call her and her mother would say she wasn't home. I would look for her in the mall and her friends would laugh at me and throw things. I went to her house, and her father chased me off like a dog. His own future son-in-law. Finally, I prayed and took counsel from my father, and I waited until school started and went and looked for her there at the high school. But her teachers told me she hadn't shown up for class. And I knew that she had run away from God. And from me."

He stood up again, his fists now clenched in front of him. His trunk-like thighs seemed to strain against his tan slacks. His striped shirt seemed about to tear at the shoulders. His head looked almost as if it would scrape the ceiling. "So I went to see her friends," he said through clenched teeth. "And they didn't laugh at me this time. No, sir. I braved them right in their lair, right in their place out by the train tracks where they sit together and smoke their unholy drugs and drink their liquor. Oh, they laughed at first. They laughed at first. But the Lord made me mighty, and I grabbed one of them—Jack Amberson, his name was—a grinning, yellow-eyed pawn of the legions—and I took him in my hands and I lifted him above my head." He raised his hands to demonstrate. I sat watching him, my eyes wide. "I lifted him and I told him if he did not tell me where Georgia had gone, I would dash him down on the ground like Moses did to the ten commandments." He lowered his hands. He seemed to come to himself. "And he told me, all right. You bet he did. He told me she'd gone away to become an actress in Los Angeles."

"So you came to New York, heard my name on the radio, and punched my lights out. It's all clear to me now."

"Huh?"

"Never mind. Go ahead."

"Well, he'd lied to me. Jack Amberson. Can you believe that? He lied just to save his miserable skin." I said I could believe it. "I bid my daddy good-bye, and I set my schooling aside, and I spent every last penny I had to travel to Los Angeles, that Sodom, that sinful city." Slowly, he sank back into his chair. "She wasn't there, Mr. Wells. I searched for her for almost three months. After that time, I received a letter from my father in the mission where I was staying. He begged me to come back, Mr. Wells. He said my name had now become a laughingstock before the people. He said it was now talked around town as common knowledge that Georgia hadn't gone to Los Angeles at all. She'd run away to become an actress. But it was New York she'd come to."

The blood left under his nose had dried to a brown scab. But now a fresh stream started running from his nostril. He sniffled and dabbed at it with his wrist. "My daddy begged me to come home," he repeated. "But he also said he'd managed to talk to Georgia's mother and she was reluctant, she said I should leave her daughter alone. But Daddy convinced her to give him Georgia's address and phone number to allow us young people to work things out by ourselves." He gave one grave nod. "That's the kind of man my daddy is, Mr. Wells. He knows a man can't just abandon his fiancée to the devil. No, sir. So I took the number and I called Georgia in New York." Now, the memory made his big head hang down. "Took me forever to reach her, then when I did . . ." His clear blue eyes misted over. "When I did, she told me it was over, Mr. Wells. Told me she'd found another man, this senator fellow, this Paul Abingdon, and that he was going to help her become famous and . . . and . . . He was married, Mr. Wells. She told me so right there on the phone." His head came up, he balled his hand into a fist. "Well, I swore to myself right then and there, I swore, 'Wally, you are going to rescue this poor sinner from the jaws of perdition if it's the last thing you do.' And I didn't have a dime either, hardly a thin dime. But I started working around the town and taking any odd job I could get me, and then I started hitching and walking and traveling any way I could to get across this country." He eyed me solemnly. "I've been in some hard-time places, Mr. Wells, and some good-time places. But now I'm here, and I'm fixing to find her."

"I thought you said your father gave you her address."

"She's not there anymore. She's moved away. I've been asking around all over town about her, everywhere I could think of to ask, I found some people—some of these actor people—who say they know her, but no one seems to know where she is."

I thought this over, smoking silently. "And when you heard about me and the pictures on the radio, you just assumed they were pictures of her?"

He nodded. "I knew that Abingdon fellow would lead her to perdition. I knew it. And when I heard that story on the radio, well, I just knew he'd done it. And I thought you . . . I don't know, I was so angry and confused . . . I guess I thought you were gonna put it in the newspaper. Tell everyone. God forgive me for turning to violence. I was just confused."

I considered his stern, bewildered, innocent face. I believed him. I rubbed the back of my neck, trying to figure out what to say. The pain in my head was subsiding to a dull throb. "Listen, pal . . . Wally," I said. "Any chance you could just turn around, go on home to Ohio? Forget about this girl? You know: finish studying to be a preacher and everything?"

His eyes widened. "I couldn't, Mr. Wells. I just couldn't. That day, that day down at Fallon's Creek . . . Why . . ." He looked for words to express the gravity of it. "Why, we got engaged."

I noticed now he hadn't touched his coffee. It reminded me of mine. I reached for it, sipped it. It was stone cold. I said: "Wally. You got laid, not engaged."

His face went blank again. "Huh?"

"There's a difference. I mean, just because you and a girl make love, have sex, whatever, doesn't mean she's gotta marry you."

"Huh?"

"Wally, what I'm trying to say is . . ." My voice trailed off. Wally stared at me. He waited for me to continue. I sighed. "Have you got a place to stay?"

"Oh yeah," he said eagerly. "St. Clement's Mission of Mercy over on Tenth Avenue. I help out with the soup kitchen and they let me sleep on a cot in the cellar."

"Great."

"Yeah." He grinned. He had dimples in both of his plump cheeks. "Yeah, I don't mind if the rats don't."

I laughed. I nodded. I glanced at my watch. "Is the day over yet?" I asked him.

"Huh?" he said.

"Never mind."

6

We walked out into the heat together. We labored through it to the local Xerox store. I had the kid run off a copy of Georgia Stuart's photograph. I told him if I came across anything, I'd give him a call, let him know. Then I thanked him for the morning's entertainment and sent him back to his mission of mercy.

I went to a phone booth. I held the receiver to my ear. My ear started sweating. I dialed, sweating. The sweat ran out of my sideburns, down my jaw. My collar grew damp with it. I called the *Star* and asked for Cambridge.

"Sorry," I said. He was silent. I sweat. "A guy hit me," I said. "You can see it. A purple bruise."

He was silent another moment. I spent the moment sweating. Then Cambridge said quietly: "The People Upstairs waited for you a half hour."

"Look, Bob, I'm sorry. I'll be there by nine-thirty."

"It's nine-thirty now."

"I'll be there by ten."

"Be in the upstairs conference room by ten-thirty."

"Count on it."

He was silent. I sweat. "Have you seen the *Post*?" he asked.

"No," I said.

"See the *Post*."

He hung up. I hung up. I wiped my face. I flicked my hand. The water shot from it in a spray. The sun beat down on me through the gray mist that would not break, that would not give up its rain. I left the booth. I headed to the newsstand. I bought the *Post*. It was out early with an extra. ABINGDON IN LOVE NEST BLACKMAIL, read the headline. The sub read: A *POST* EXCLUSIVE: HOW *STAR* REPORTER GOT SCOOPED ON HIS OWN STORY.

I retrieved the Artful Dodge from its cave. I headed downtown. I sweat.

When I came into the city room, I noticed a certain pall had descended on the place. There was more than one dour face among the regulars and I saw a few of my colleagues cast doleful looks my way. When I passed Rafferty walking through the maze of white walls to my desk, he tightened his lips and slapped me on the shoulder. Alice Pucci, from fashion, called "Good luck, John," as I went by her. Fran came running up to me with a cup of coffee. She thrust it soulfully into my hands, then she turned and hurried away.

By the time I reached my cubicle I was almost in mourning myself. I found McKay sitting in my chair. Lansing was sitting on my desk. They got to their feet when I came in.

"What the hell happened to your face?" Lansing asked.

"I got punched."

"The meeting hasn't even started yet."

"I was practicing. Excuse me."

I pushed past McKay. I sat down in my swivel chair. I leaned back and lifted my feet on the filing cabinet. I rested my coffee on my belt buckle, fumbled a cigarette between my teeth.

"Oh," said McKay, covering his mouth, "I'll always remember him that way." He crinkled up his eyes like he was crying.

"Knock it off," Lansing said.

"Here," McKay said abruptly. He shoved a five-spot at me. "I owe you this. I never paid it back."

I considered the five. "You don't owe me that."

"Take it. Take it. I want to pay it back anyway. And Mrs. Mac wants you to come to dinner on Friday. Saturday, too."

I laughed. "Shut up," I said. I lit my cigarette.

McKay shrugged, stuffed the bill into his shirt. "You know Gershon is giving odds on this meeting. At eight o'clock, it was three to one you wouldn't come out employed. Now it's five to one you won't come out alive."

"Can you get me a piece of that?"

"Which angle?"

Lansing leaned against the wall. One corner of her mouth lifted. "You know it's not really all that goddamned funny."

"Are you going to start this again?"

She thought about it. "No. I guess not. But what I don't think I can forgive you for is making Cambridge this happy." She sat on my desk again. "He's been walking around here all morning. . . . He's been trying to look stern and angry. But every now and again, you can just see it. That grin hiding underneath." She looked at me. Her mouth was still smiling a little, but her eyes were dead serious. "He's got you where he wants you, you know."

"Maybe."

"Not maybe."

"Maybe," I said.

"You don't understand. You think, oh, you're the best, you've kept them ahead on every metro scandal story in the past eighteen months. You think that gives you some kind of leverage over a fluff king like Cambridge." She shook her head. "It won't buy you the time of day on this one, old friend. You blew this one, and this one's different. This isn't just some minor scandal you got scooped on. This isn't just pols ripping off the public or stealing from the poor or squeezing a union till the members bleed. This is sex, Wells. They know how to spell this one. They know what it means. And they'll never forgive you for letting it get away."

I took a long drag on my cigarette. I said: "Maybe."

But Lansing didn't let up. She couldn't. Anger pushed her on. I could feel it steaming. She was still mad at me and she wanted to make this hurt. "You know where I was this morning at nine o'clock?"

"I guess you'll tell me."

"I guess I will. I was at Christian Maldonado's campaign headquarters."

I blinked. "You're joking."

"He called a press conference."

"On this?"

"He wanted to assure the good people of New York State that, as a family man, he has never compromised his integrity in a way that might leave him open to blackmail."

I snorted. "A family man. Did he mention that it's the Dellacroce family? That guy's been mob since he was low-balling garbage contracts for Westchester County. He's one of the guys who had my car blown up that time." Lansing raised her eyes to heaven. "He did," I said. "And I'd have had him indicted too except my source—this county clerk—what was his name? Clark Warner, poor guy. He's driving home from work one summer evening and there's this pickup in front of him with some rolled up carpet in back of it. Suddenly, the carpet bounces off the truck, crashes through the windshield of Clark's car and smashes him right in the face. Crushed his head. Blew his brains out both ears. And put a real dent in my story. Christian Maldonado. Mr. Morality. I remember the next day I asked Maldonado if his carpet ever arrived. They had to pull him away from me." I chuckled at the memory. Lansing did not chuckle at the memory. "I guess that was before your time," I said.

"It was ten years ago. For the last five years, he's been an assemblyman and no one's had a bad word to say about him."

"No one whose body has been found."

"And now he's got his opponent smeared all over the front page," Lansing said. "Not our front page, mind you. But let's just call it the figurative front page."

"Wait a minute," said McKay. "You can't blame Wells for smearing Abingdon and for getting scooped at the same time. I mean, if he'd gotten the story then Ab . . . then he . . . Abing . . ."

His argument collapsed under the weight of Lansing's glare. He fell silent.

"That's telling her, Mac," I said.

"Hey, Lansing," someone shouted. "Your mother on line eight."

"What is this?" I said. "Mother's Day all week?"

"Listen," Lansing explained, "shut the hell up." She strode off to her cubicle to take the call.

I looked at my watch.

"It's time, son," McKay said. " 'Tis a far, far better thing you do than you have ever done. 'Tis a far, far better place you go to than you have ever known."

I dug my ashtray out of the desk debris. I put out my cigarette. I stood up. I dusted off my jacket. "How do I look?"

"Like incipient dog meat."

I glanced over toward Lansing's cubicle. She was standing in the aisle, I could see her. She was talking into the phone. Gesturing with her hands. She put her fist to her hip. Her cheeks were red.

"You know," I said. "I don't think she's all right."

McKay watched her for a moment, too. "She's ticked about something, all right. Maybe it's a guy."

"Nah," I said. "She wouldn't get that crazy over a guy."

McKay shrugged.

"Nah," I said again. I laid my hand on my stomach. "You think Cambridge will bring in Danish for this one?"

"Iranians," McKay said. "The Danish aren't that good with guns."

I marched off to meet my fate.

7

It was not a far, far better place I went to than I had ever known. Hell, I had known plenty of far, far better places. This was just another conference room, though it was a little ritzier than the last one I'd been in. This one had a window, for instance. It looked out on the white heat misting over the Pan Am Building. It also had a shag carpet, tan, no cigarette holes. And the long table at the center of it was made out of real wood, oak I think, not the linoleum reserved for the staff. The swivel chairs around the table were plusher. So were the people in them.

There were four people in them. One of them was Cambridge. The other three were The People Upstairs. They were sitting there, waiting for me, when I came into the room. Cambridge was closest to the door. Farthest, that is, from the seat of power at the opposite head of the table. He was sitting, hunched forward over his yellow legal pad. He wore a pale green suit without a wrinkle on it. It looked like the skin of a seasick infant. He brushed at his hair with his fingers, looking serious and concerned.

The man seated next to him was Max Hodgekiss, our editor-in-chief. He was around fifty, short and slim, dressed in impeccable dark gray. He was bald except for a fringe of white, impeccably clipped. He had a round, small, impeccable face with impeccably tight lips. He didn't know anything, and he had no power.

In the chair across from him was Roy Sandler, our executive editor. He was also about fifty, short and slim, but he was nowhere near impeccable. In fact, there was something almost feral about him. He had a bullet head, crisscrossed with black hairs. He had heavy eyebrows over deepset eyes. The eyes were sharp and hungry. They kept moving. They devoured what they touched and then passed on. Sandler had power all right. At times, he ran the place. He liked me, too, as much as he liked anybody. We understood each other.

Finally, at the head of the table, was the King himself. Our publisher, Milton Bush. He was a big old son of a gun was Milton. He was big and broad and he pushed against his gray pinstriped vest like an expanding balloon. He had a full head of hair. It was gray and it was cut short. He had a face that came at you like the front end of a locomotive. There was a slight, cruel smile stuck on his pale, thin lips. He looked like he was daring you to stand in his way.

Bush and I had only met a few times. He always tried to break a bone or two when he shook my hand, but it was nothing personal. I'd heard all the scuttlebutt on him—his mistreated wife, his well-kept mistresses, his vicious tactics in the boardroom and so on. I'd heard he once voted a rival's job away while the guy was in the john. But that was just secondhand stuff. It had nothing to do with me.

My position with him was hard to figure. He knew I was a good reporter. He'd said so to my face. He knew I'd kept the *Star* on top during the recent scandals, and that our circulation had risen during those scandals, leaving the competition in the dust. So that counted in my favor. Against me, though, was Bush himself; the man, his personality. It was my guess that he was the kind of guy who didn't much care what else I could do as long as I could touch the floor with my nose. If I could do that every now and again about two inches in front of his polished black oxfords, then I'd be all right. That was my strategy anyway: bow, scrape, eat shit and go back to work.

I inclined my head toward the four of them. "Gentlemen," I said.

Cambridge pretended not to know me. He hardly looked up. Bush just sort of snorted in derision.

"Come on in, John," Sandler said. "Sit down."

I sat down at the head of the table, opposite Bush. There were ashtrays all around. I pulled one toward me. Cambridge gave me a look. I lit a cigarette. Bush cleared his throat, reached into his pocket and hauled out a cigar the size of my arm. Cambridge looked down again. I sat back, took a drag and waited.

Sandler glanced at Bush. Bush nodded. Sandler said, "John . . ." He had a hard, sharp voice. "John, we don't want you to feel that you're on trial here. We know how much you mean to this newspaper. We respect that. But . . . We don't much like being made a laughingstock. You've seen the *Post*, I imagine."

I nodded. "Yeah, I've seen it."

"Well, you can see how we feel. I mean, we know that mistakes can happen. We'd just like to hear from you exactly how it did happen, and hear any ideas you might have for getting back on top of this story."

I opened my mouth to speak.

"I think what Roy is saying," said Hodgekiss. He leaned forward to illustrate with an open hand. "Is: we want your version of the story, and any solutions you might have for what's gone wrong."

My mouth was still open. I put my cigarette in it, sucked in some smoke. "Two nights ago," I said, "Mayforth Kendrick called me up. Said he had a story for me. It was slow, I figured I'd check it out. I went to his apartment and he showed me photographs of Paul Abingdon having sex with a woman I'd never seen before. . . ."

"Excuse me for interrupting. . . ." Hodgekiss leaned forward. "But was this . . . normal sex?"

"What?"

"Because we've heard rumors now that he was engaged in something offbeat. Out of the way. Uh—you know . . ."

Now Hodgekiss used his hand to make circular you-know motions in the air.

I used my hand to scratch my nose. "He tied her hands with a belt or something and hit her with this scarf she had."

"Ah. Ah," said our editor-in-chief, nodding vigorously. "I see. Okay. Fine. Now I see."

"So anyway . . ." I said.

"Fine," said Hodgekiss. "Go ahead. Okay."

"Anyway, Kendrick hinted he'd tried to blackmail Abingdon with the photos, but Abingdon wouldn't bite, so he was trying to sell them to me." I faltered. I took a deep breath.

"Uh—what did you do, John?" Sandler asked.

I looked him dead in the eye. "I said it was no story. I turned him down."

Sandler smiled softly. He nodded. He lowered his head. On my right, Cambridge bent over his legal pad, trying not to dance and sing for joy. Next to him, Hodgekiss made vague exclamations under his breath. Bush just stared at me. He had a stare that hit you like a Giants linebacker.

"Why, John?" Sandler asked. "Why'd you turn him down?"

I gestured with the cigarette. "Like I said. It's no story. Not unless his private life affects his public action."

"It's sure a story now," said Cambridge. He laughed. He looked at everyone else to see if they laughed. They smiled. He stopped laughing and smiled instead.

"You're right," I said. "It is. But at the time, I didn't know Kendrick was going to get murdered. It didn't come up."

One by one, starting with Bush, the smiles faded away. The room was silent. So far, Bush had held his cigar in his hand unlit. Now he stuck the monster in his face. He torched it with a sleek lighter of gold. He puffed great gobs of green smoke. The silence continued. So did the smoke. It billowed out over our heads and hung there in a thin layer. So did the silence.

Then, in a voice like a cannon shot, Bush said, "What I'd like to know is: Where the fuck do you get off making a decision like that without consulting your superior, without consulting Cambridge?"

"Well, sir, after twenty-six years as a reporter I . . ."

"I don't give diddly shit about your twenty-six years as a reporter, Wells. The reporters who work for me don't make decisions like that. We hire people to make those decisions. People with brains."

My breath held itself. I felt the blood pounding in my brows. Beside me, Cambridge was nodding sagely, solemnly. Only the light in his eyes was dancing.

I ran a finger across the top of my lip. It came away damp. I looked at Bush with his big chest thrown out toward me. "Well, sir," I said softly, "maybe you're right."

"Right?" Bush stared at Sandler for a second as if to assure himself he'd heard me. Next he stared at me. He sat forward with his hands folded together to do it. The cigar stuck up between the fingers of one of the hands. "You're damned right I'm right," he said. "I know I'm right. And this may come as a surprise to you, but I don't need a fifty-year-old street reporter to tell me I'm right."

I didn't have to take that. "Forty-six," I said, and I put some spin on it too.

Bush pushed his big face at me with its thin and nasty smile. "Forty-six." He nodded. "And when you're fifty, you'll still be a street reporter. If you're lucky."

I finally took a breath. It wasn't much as breaths go. The blood hammered in my head even louder. My chest felt like someone had tied a knot in it. "Well, sir," I said softly, "maybe you're right."

Cambridge kept looking at his legal pad. His expression hadn't changed. But his cheeks had turned the color of the sunset in Jersey—a deep scarlet. It was, I guessed, the unmistakeable sign that he was having a meaningful sensual experience.

And it wasn't over yet.

"Now," said Bush. He sat back in his chair. He cocked his cigar at the ceiling. He smiled at me. Snakes smile that way when they unhinge their jaws. "Since it didn't occur to you to ask your superior what to do in the first place, maybe it would help you to have him explain to you now the exact extent of the damage you've caused us."

He looked at Cambridge. Sandler looked at Cambridge. Hodgekiss cleared his throat and looked at Cambridge.

Cambridge adjusted his tie. He lifted the top page on his legal pad to consult the notes beneath. I didn't think he would be able to look me in the eye. But I was wrong. He'd waited two years for this. He wasn't going to miss it.

He looked me in the eye. "John," he said gently, smoothly. "I just want to reiterate what Roy here has said. We want you to know—I personally want you to know—that you're not on trial here or, you know, under the gun in any way. We're just trying to give you the kind of useful constructive criticism that will improve your performance in the future. Now, do you understand that?"

I couldn't speak. I forced myself to nod.

Cambridge raised his index finger. He placed it thoughtfully against his lower lip. "You see," he said, "when someone comes to you with a story like this one, and you turn it down on your own initiative, you take an important decision out of management's hands. I mean, out of the hands of the very people who are paid to make decisions like that and who might be able to make them with a cooler head than the reporter on the scene. Now, in this case, for instance, you saw some pictures, they were distasteful, you thought forget it, and now you've got every paper in town ahead of us on our own story. Okay? That's number one."

Cambridge lowered his index finger to consult his notes again. When he looked up, he looked me in the eye again. I gained a moment by crushing out my cigarette, but he waited until I met his gaze. I did. I looked right into his eyes. I could feel sweat breaking out on my forehead. I cursed myself for it.

"Second," Cambridge said, "you turned your back on a political story with major ramifications, leaving us open to attacks of partisanship. Third, you made a value judgment instead of a news judgment that I just don't think was justified."

"What Bob is saying," broke in Hodgekiss, out of pure stupidity I imagine, "is: despite its decidedly controversial or you might say explicit or sexual nature, this is definitely in my judgment, and I'm sure in the judgment of Mr. Bush here a legitimate, a decidedly legitimate news story."

I swiped at the sweat on my brow as inconspicuously as I could. "Well, sir," I said gently, "maybe you're right."

Cambridge was about to start in again, but Hodgekiss was encouraged and went on. "You know, we've discussed this very thoroughly upstairs here, and it seems to us that pictures like these say something very definite about a candidate's character."

"Definitely," said Cambridge, slicing the air with the edge of his hand. "Definitely, definitely. There is no question about it. This is a character issue. This is not the first time Abingdon has done this. It's a real, a real habit with him. And it's something the public definitely, definitely, definitely has a right to know. I mean, this is a man who wants to be a senator, a man who one day may try to become president. I mean, you essentially, when you turned those pictures down, you just threw morality out the window. You took the first amendment into your own hands."

"And I'll tell you something else," said Bush. He leaned forward again, this time to jab his cigar at me. "I'll tell you something else. By turning down those pictures, you put us in a situation where the next time someone has something like this to offer, they may not come to us first. They may say to themselves, 'Oh—huh!—The *Star*! That's that paper with . . . integrity!' " He spoke the last word with a single explosion of laughter. It was echoed by the other three. He pointed the cigar again. "I don't need integrity, Wells. I need news. Do you understand me?"

I stalled. I reached for a cigarette. I brought it to my lips. My hands were trembling. I wondered if they could see that. I lit a match and held it to the cigarette's tip. I watched Bush through the flame. He was leaning toward me, waiting.

"Do you understand?" he said again.

I waved out the match. The sweat that had gathered on my forehead finally fell. A drop of it rolled down the side of my jaw.

I tried to speak. I was too hoarse. I had to clear my throat. Finally, I got it out.

"Well, sir," I said gently, "you are full of shit."

I took a breath of smoke. I blew the smoke out. No one said anything. The four men looked at me, as if they were still waiting for me to speak, as if they had decided to discount what they had just heard and start the moment over again at the beginning.

I wiped the sweat off my forehead with the heel of my trembling hand.

"John," said Sandler. "Let's try and deal with this in a measured . . ."

"Wait a minute," said Bush. "Wait a minute. Did you just tell me I'm full of shit?"

"Yeah," I said. I shook my head sadly. "Yeah, damn it, I did." I could feel my heartbeat beginning to slow. I could feel the sweat drying on my brow. I had surely lost my job. The sudden freedom rolled over me like a wave. "And you are, too," I added carelessly, "completely full of shit."

Bush laughed. It was not an I-like-your-spirit-son laugh. It was an oh-good-meat-for-supper laugh. He waved his cigar at me gracefully. "All right," he said in great good humor. "All right, suppose you explain to me how I'm full of shit."

I considered it for a drag or two. "Well. Just on the face of it, for instance," I said. "You say these photographs say a lot about Abingdon's character. And they do, all right. That's certain. But so do his fantasies, his private thoughts,

the notes of his clergyman or his psychiatrist. All that stuff
says a lot about his character. But it says it in a way that is
not within our purview. Anymore than your fantasies or
thoughts or psychiatrist's notes are within our purview." I
smoked. I thought. "What else?" I said. "You say the public
has a right to know because the man is asking to be a senator.
Okay. That's a job. The public hires him to do it. That's
what a campaign is: it's a job interview with the public.
They have the right to hire him or not, but they have no
right to pry into his private life anymore than their bosses
should pry into theirs. If they do hire him and they don't
like the way he does his job, they can fire him. If he breaks
the law while he does it, he should be put in jail like anyone
else. We report to the public on his public conduct so they
can make those decisions. When his public conduct goes
astray, we have a right to know why, whether it's incom-
petence or greed or a love affair or whatever. But as for his
private morality, you're right: I throw it out the window. I
couldn't care less. If I knew one damn thing about morality,
I'd be in a different business anyway." I leveled my cigarette
at Bush where he sat back smiling and puffing smoke. "But
that's not why you're full of shit," I said.

Sandler shook his head, rubbed his eyes with the fingers
of one hand. Hodgekiss sat frozen, his head tilted to one
side, his mouth open, his eyes gazing into space blankly.
Cambridge stared at me. His lip curled. It occurred to me
suddenly that he was truly disgusted by my conduct on this
story. He was an idiot.

As for Bush, he simply nodded at me without removing
the cigar from his mug. "Go on," he said.

"The reason you're full of shit," I said, "is because you
don't care. Not really. You don't really give a damn about
any of it. You care about getting the circulation, and you
care about having the sex in your pages, and you care about
having the power to make powerful people twist and grovel
and sweat and fall down. But a job exists for a reason, and
the reason my job exists is to tell people some of what's

going on in the world so they can decide if they want to do something about it. And you don't care a rat's ass about that and never have. Before I picked up a phone to call one of you people for editorial guidance in the field, I'd do something really radical and phone Rafferty, who happens to be the city editor and the guy I'm answerable to in these situations. I'd call him and he'd tell me to make my own decision like the veteran I am and leave him the fuck alone." I laughed. I waved off the lot of them. "Just tell me when I've lost my job, okay, because I don't want to talk to you guys any longer than I have to."

That made Cambridge look eagerly at Bush. Bush still chomped, still puffed, still stared at me. The long wait was supposed to make me sweat and tremble with anxiety. It didn't. I'd reached my limit. Bush was tough, all right. Tough and powerful. He could take my job without blinking and he could eat my future, such as it was, and spit it out. But I didn't give a damn about that just then. I'd had it.

While the others watched, he plucked the cigar from his mouth. Daintily. Like picking a rose. He examined the smoldering tip of it. "Let me ask you something, Mr. Wells," he said to it. "I'm not exactly clear on this. Am I supposed to admire your courage?"

I shoved my chair back and stood up. "I don't care what you do. I rode into this state in a boxcar, pal, and if I have to, I'll ride out again the same goddamn way."

He nodded slowly. "Well, I'm giving you the rest of the week to break this story open," he said. "Get the pictures first, find the girl. I don't care what. Just put us back on top of it." He rotated his hand, examined his watch. "This is Thursday. You have until Monday's editions to put us out in front. If you don't, you're fired. If we get scooped again on it, you're not only fired . . ." He raised his eyes from his watch to me. ". . . I'll pick out the boxcar."

My lips parted. I was surprised. I had been mentally counting up my savings to see how long I could last on unemployment. I had not expected a reprieve. For a second

or two, all I could do was stand there staring at Bush. I had
no idea what was going on in the guy's mind. I wasn't going
to ask.

I tipped a finger at the man. I bowed my head to the
rest of them. First Sandler, then Hodgekiss, then Cambridge. Cambridge was still trying to look smug, but I noticed a faint tinge of green had crept in under his flush.

I left him there. I walked out of the room. I shut the
door behind me. I leaned against the wall, listening to the
hammer of my heart.

8

I walked back into the city room. I tried not to look pale. I wasn't very good at it. As I walked through the maze of white partitions, every eye in every cubicle I passed turned up to look at me. Some of those eyes held pity in them. Some held bitter joy. I walked by all of them until I reached my desk. I sat down. I lit a cigarette. I stared at the rubbish piled up in front of me. I wished I had a door to close.

"How bad?" It was McKay. He leaned against the edge of the entrance. His baby face was puckered with concern.

I kept staring at the garbage heap of crumbled papers and ashes and pencils without points. It looked good to me. I had been with the *Star* eleven years. I liked it here. More than I wanted to admit.

I took a deep breath. "Bad," I said.

McKay got hoarse suddenly. "You out?"

I shook my head. "Not yet."

"That's good anyway."

"Yeah, I guess."

"You don't sound sure."

I kept staring, kept shaking my head. "I'm not sure." I scratched the side of my head. "I don't even know how it happened. Or why."

"Well, I'm glad to have you around anyway. Can I have my five dollars back?"

"Yeah sure." I took out a wallet and wrenched out a fiver. I gave it to him.

"Thanks," he said. He stuffed it in his pocket. He gave me a jaunty wave. He started back to his desk.

"Wait a minute," I said. "What five dollars?"

"Oh by the way," McKay called. "Lansing said to wish you luck whatever happens."

"Where is she, anyway?" I called back. "Don't I even rate a condolence call?"

"She waited as long as she could. She just headed out to Abingdon's press conference."

I shot out of my chair. "Is she gone?"

McKay shrugged. "She just left."

I took off. I wove past the cubicle partitions to the glass doors. I had five days to get this story, and Abingdon's press conference was a good place to start.

I pushed out into the elevator lobby.

"Christ," I said. I had forgotten about the heat. It coiled around my skin like a snake.

I got in the elevator and rode down, hoping to catch Lansing outside.

I caught her all right. As I came out the front door, I saw her sitting in her red sports car. It was parked at the curb. I hurried toward it along the sidewalk, fighting against the thickness of the heat. When I came up to the passenger window, I saw that Lansing was just sitting behind the wheel. Just sitting there, staring. There was a tear rolling down her fine high cheek. I was so startled that for a second I couldn't even retreat. But she didn't see me, she didn't turn around.

She reached forward suddenly, almost angrily. She grabbed hold of the key in the ignition. She wrenched it to one side. The little sports car coughed, then roared, then screeched as she kept holding the key down and the starter scraped.

I backed up a few steps. "Hey, Lansing, wait," I called to her.

She glanced around quickly. When she saw it was me, she swiped at her cheek with one hand. By the time I leaned down at the window, she could pass.

"Can I bum a lift?" I asked.

She nodded. "Get in."

I slid in next to her. We took off. We rode down through the narrow lane of Vanderbilt to Forty-second Street. We curled around to Park and headed downtown. The finely shaped apartment buildings rose up on either side of us. The avenue's center islands were pink with begonias.

Lansing didn't talk for the first few minutes. I tried not to look at her too closely. I fiddled with the air-conditioning vents for a while. After that, I just peered out the window.

Finally, she said: "So? Should I drop you at the unemployment office?"

"Ha ha."

"You survived then?" Her voice was a little thick, but that was all.

"For now, anyway," I said.

There was a pause. She said: "I'm glad."

The way she said it, I had to turn to her. She glanced over at me and smiled.

She looked fine now. She looked better than fine. She looked fresh again and beautiful, the way she looked sometimes when she first came into the city room in the morning. You'd be sitting at your desk staring into your coffee and you'd see her and feel better about it all. Sometimes I would think about that look when I was away from her. Sometimes when I was sitting in a bar watching a Mets game. Or when I was sitting home alone watching the glow of the neon lights from the theater across the street. I would think about it, and then I would stop thinking about it. Lansing was twenty years younger than I was. She was pretty and smart, and I was old and ugly. The last thing she needed was to have me sitting at home thinking about how she looked in the morning.

We hit Thirty-sixth, turned left. Headed down a hill lined with brownstones. In front of us, the street broadened as it was joined by other streets and avenues. Then all of them funneled down into the Midtown Tunnel. We went down

with them. We raced into the long tube of red taillights
and yellow tiles.

We drove without speaking. I smoked and thought. I
thought about Bush. I couldn't figure out what he was up
to. I couldn't figure out what he wanted to prove. He had
a rep as the kind of guy who would crush you for nothing.
Why had he let me slap at him like that and get away?

It made me nervous. I tried to figure it. The yellow tiles
of the tunnel rushed by me in a blur.

Then Lansing cleared her throat and said: "So uh . . .
Abingdon . . . I never covered him before. Anything I should
know?"

I shrugged. "Wear a scarf if you date him."

"What?"

"No. You know. Nothing much. The usual Kennedy type."

She gave a little laugh. "Sometimes I think Kennedy
wasn't killed. I think he was shattered into little pieces and
each piece grew into a whole new candidate."

"That's Abingdon, all right. From Massachusetts and
everything. Somerville. Except he wasn't rich. He had one
of those mothers, you know, who work their fingers to the
bone to make it happen for their sons. She was a secretary,
I think, and took in sewing or something. That's the official
line, anyway. Sent him to Princeton, too."

Lansing whistled.

"Yeah," I said. "Then Harvard Law on a scholarship and
after that, it was JFK all the way. Activist law. Fought off
some big highway project that would have displaced a bunch
of poor folk. Pictures of him on TV with his jacket off and
his tie loosened and his sleeves rolled up. All that . . ." I
gestured to the gray peak high on my forehead. "And hair,
too. And the wife always standing next to him smiling."

"What's her name?"

"Jane. Skinny, high cheekbones. New Englander. Real
fierce and moral. A Katharine Hepburn type. They got into
politics in the seventies. They'd left Massachusetts by that
time. Too overcrowded with pols. They came to New York,

worked on a few campaigns, then went on to the state assembly for a term. Then Congress. And he's done pretty well, too. Liberal. A lot of housing protection stuff, anti-discrimination. He's been fine."

"Ah," she said. "But has he been good?"

From the end of the tunnel, the gray light of Queens rushed toward us. It grew brighter. We broke out into it. We coasted to a stop at a tollbooth. Lansing tossed about forty dollars in change into the electric basket. She hit the pedal and we rolled off down the Long Island Expressway.

"Has he?" she repeated.

"Been good? Apparently, he's been very, very good."

"Ha ha."

"Too good for his own good. That's his reputation anyway."

The world opened up around us. The hot gray sky flagged above low brick buildings. The sky and the buildings stretched out to the horizon.

Lansing kept her eyes on the road, but she was listening carefully.

"I never covered the man," I went on. "But you know my buddy McMahon up in Albany? He covered him for the *Times-Union*. The word is, yeah, Abingdon's a lover-boy. He's handsome and he's headed for the top and it's easy for him and he uses it. Frequently. With anything that happens to be wearing a skirt. McMahon says he and a couple of other capitol boys got drunk one night and made a pool on it. They took turns tagging after the guy for a week to see how many senators' wives and secretaries and local weather girls he could hit. Whoever got the number within ten took the pot."

"I get the picture," said Lansing. "And what about our fierce and moral Katharine Hepburn type?"

"Well, there are two versions of that, and I guess either of them could be true. One story has it that she was never much for that sort of thing. She is kind of dried up and, I don't know, ferociously noble, if you get what I mean. So she had her two kids, one boy and one girl, and gave the good congressman his freedom."

"Why does she stay?"

"Ambition, or maybe because she can accomplish the things that matter to her more easily being a congressman's wife."

Lansing chewed it over a few seconds. "This sounds suspiciously like the male version," she said. "What's the real one?"

I laughed. "Okay. The other story is that his screwing around broke her proud, stern and moral heart. When she found out about it, she left him. She went away for a few weeks—supposedly on vacation but, in fact, to carry on a tortured conversation with her God and soul. How's this one?"

"Better."

"I thought you'd like it. Anyway, after said tortured conversation with the aforementioned God and soul, she decided her noble goals and/or political ambitions could best be served by returning to her work, husband and children. But the cost has been that dried-up, ferocious nobility of hers."

"Because she really loved him once."

"So the story goes."

She was quiet a while. She ran her fingers back through her hair. Her hair ran out behind her, silken and blond. The motion cleared her cheek, the cheek where her tear had been. I studied the smoothness of the skin there, its faint flush.

This time, she did glance over. She saw me looking. The flush deepened.

"Stop looking at me that way, Wells," she said, smiling.

"That's my line, isn't it?"

She stopped smiling. "Yeah." She turned back to the road. The highway was uncrowded and we cruised on quickly. Trees grew out of the stone, grass grew up around the houses. We were in the suburbs at the borough's edge.

I leaned toward her. "Listen . . ." I began.

"So is Abingdon aiming at the White House?" she asked me.

I hesitated. I leaned back in my seat. I lit a fresh cigarette. "Yeah," I said. "Yeah, he was."

"Why was? You think this'll stop him?"

I shrugged. "Hard to know."

"I guess a lot depends on whether they find Kendrick's pictures."

I reached into my jacket pocket. I felt the piece of paper in there: the copy of Wally Shakespeare's photograph of Georgia Stuart.

"Yeah," I said. "And on who finds them first."

9

Paul Abingdon's house sat on a hill. The house was imitation Tudor. The hill was real grass, sweetly green. There were maples on the hill. They were tall and majestic. They were full with summer leaves. The leaves hung limp in the wet heat.

The hill rolled gracefully down to the suburban street below. The street went curling off through a quiet neighborhood of lawns and manses. Every inch of the curb, as far as the eye could see, was lined with cars. A lot of battered station wagons from the TV and radio stations. One white sound truck for a possible live spot on the noon news.

The house itself was besieged by reporters. They'd gathered on the gentle slope in a semicircle. The arc was about fifteen journalists long and three deep. It began in the pachysandra under the living room window. It curled around and ended in the holly bush outside the den. Its center was the single step before the front door where Abingdon was going to appear. The reporters' cameras, microphones and attention were all directed toward that empty step.

Lansing and I found a place to put the car about two blocks away from the house. We had to walk back up the hill. I had to push on my knees to convince them to take it. My jacket was off by that time. My tie was undone. My shirt was gray with sweat. Lansing pranced ahead of me. She moved on those long legs like a deer. Every so often, she had to stop and wait for me to catch up. Then she had to wait for me to wheeze for a few seconds before I could go on.

Finally, we came over the rise. We approached the reporters on the lawn.

"There he is," someone said.

I raised my dripping face to the front door. I expected to see Abingdon appear. Instead, I saw the semicircle of reporters spin about. In a single motion, the mob came down the hill toward me. Lansing was pushed back. The reporters closed in. A few shoved mikes under my nose. A few more pointed cameras into my face.

"John," shouted someone. "John, can you confirm for us the story about the photographs?"

I followed the voice. It was a kid I didn't know. One of the TV girls. Where the hell did she get off calling me John?

"Do you know the identity of the woman?" someone else shouted.

I looked for him, but before I could find him, someone else pressed close with a microphone.

"Why did you refuse to report the existence of the pictures before Kendrick's death?"

"Do you feel you've been scooped on your own story?"

"What was your relationship with Kendrick?"

"Don't the people have the right to know about their candidates, Mr. Wells?"

I waited. The questions started to run out of steam. They stopped. I smiled. I grinned. I laughed.

I reached into my pants pocket. The nearest reporter to me was Molly Caldwell from CNC-TV. She was a striking woman. Small and thin with a cap of black hair. She pushed her microphone toward me. I brought a quarter and a dime up and handed it to her. Surprised, she took it.

"Buy the *Star* tomorrow and read all about it," I said.

There was a collective groan. It was followed by angry shouts.

"You're a reporter—"

"The people have a right to know—"

"You have an ethical responsibility—"

Nothing is as ethical as a reporter who hasn't gotten what he wants.

"That's S-T-A-R," I told them when the shouting died down. "Our slogan is: We tell you everything you need to know."

They were about to start in on me again. But just then, there was a noise from the house behind them. The mob swiveled away from me to regroup around the front step. My hands in my pockets, I strolled over and stood behind them. Lansing came up beside me.

"That ought to keep Bush happy for a while," she whispered.

"What a man will do to keep his job," I said.

The oaken door above the step had opened. Now the screen door beyond it pushed out. Two big men came through. They wore dark suits. They wore sunglasses. Their hair was clipped short. It was so black it seemed blue, like in the comics. They posted themselves on either side of the step and crossed their arms on their expansive chests. Abingdon's bodyguards.

Next came the candidate and his wife. He opened the door for her. A perfect gentleman. Mrs. Abingdon came gingerly out onto the step. She was wearing a modest brown skirt that ended at her calves and a high-collared blouse that ended at her throat. She was very long and very skinny. Her face was all angles: sharp nose, sharp chin. Her hair, black with elegant flecks of gray, was done up in a tight bun high at the back of her head. She stood erect, her hands folded before her. She smiled, a little tightly. She posed without moving as the cameras snapped and whirred.

Her husband joined her. He came out the door and squeezed her upper arm in greeting, as if they'd just met. She turned her head and smiled at him, turned back to us. He smiled at her, turned back to us and smiled. It was all very nicely done.

The cameras kept snapping and whirring. A few reporters shouted questions. Paul Abingdon waited, turning this way and that to give all the photographers a good angle of him. All the angles were pretty good. He was a handsome man. Tall with broad shoulders and a trim waist. His hair was light brown, sculpted to his head. His face was chiseled, bronze and strong. He had piercing blue eyes, and a jutting jaw. He was thirty-six or so, but when he smiled, he looked much younger, almost like a boy.

He was wearing a polo shirt and slacks, and, as I stood there bathed in sweat, I wondered how he managed to look so crisp. The heat did not seem to affect him at all.

He held up his hand. The scattered questions ceased. "I'll be brief," he said in his broad Boston twang. "I know it's hot. But if you think it's hot for you . . ."

The reporters got it after a moment and laughed. Mrs. Abingdon laughed, bending forward with it a bit.

The congressman grinned. "Actually, what I have to say is very simple. This morning, a sordid story was reported about me in some of the media. The story said that a low-level criminal had been murdered, and that he had been in possession of photographs of me with a woman." He swept over us with his piercing blue eyes. His musical drawl continued. "My comment to you on that is this: the story isn't true. Those pictures do not exist. It is not possible for them to exist. And that's all there is to say."

The questions came at once. "Are you saying you've never been unfaithful to your wife?"

Jane Abingdon lost her smile a little, but Paul actually chuckled. "My wife and I have always been quite satisfied with each other," he said. He put his arm around her shoulders.

The reporter tried to ask the question again, but it was drowned out by others.

"Do you have any information about Mayforth Kendrick's death?"

"None whatsoever," said Abingdon. "I never knew the man."

"Have you been in touch with the police?"

"Yes. I told them exactly what I've told you."

"Do you think this will hurt your campaign?"

He let his wife go, spread his arms, grinned. "Look, it's not gonna help, but it's untrue, and I feel certain it'll die down."

"How do you feel about this, Mrs. Abingdon?"

Jane kept smiling. Her eyes kept beaming. Her voice rang out high and hard and chill as a Maine morning. She even sounded like Katharine Hepburn.

"I have lived with my husband for, oh, some dozen years now." She took hold of his arm. "I haven't let him get away yet, and I don't plan to. All I want for him, for myself, and for this country, is to see Paul Abingdon in the Senate."

That stopped them for a split second. No one could think of a follow-up. She pretty well had it covered.

So they turned back to the candidate again. And someone—a man not far from me—shouted:

"Congressman—do you think John Wells lied?"

The other reporters listened. They wanted the answer to this one. Abingdon had to think for a second, but they were more than willing to wait. The candidate gazed over our heads looking inspired while he figured out what he wanted to say. I watched him. I sweat. I was getting very tired of sweating today.

"I paid close attention to what the police told me," Abingdon said. "And I can confirm your reports that these stories came from the reporter at the *Star*. Now, I don't know Mr. Wells personally, but I can only imagine that either he has been—uh—duped in some way, or that he has a reason of his own to make up a story like this."

A few reporters shouted questions together, drowning each other out. It was at that moment that Molly Caldwell got a bright idea. I don't think she'd liked my little trick with the thirty-five cents. There was a thin, wicked little smile on her red lips when she said: "Would you like to ask Mr. Wells what that reason was, Congressman? He's right here."

My heart jumped. I felt Lancer's hand on my arm. Fortunately, though, I saw my fear reflected in Abingdon's eyes. He wanted no part of a confrontation like that. It could only be messy.

He grinned, as if he hadn't heard the question. He lifted his hand in a wave.

"Well," he said, "thank you very much for coming. That's all I have time for right now. Back to the race!"

He turned away from the chorus of shouted questions. The two bodyguards closed ranks in front of him. This time, Abingdon barely had the patience to hold the door for his wife. He opened it just a crack, and she slipped in past him. The shouted questions followed, but Abingdon was quickly gone. The bodyguards stood there together for another moment, their shoulders touching, their hands folded in front of them. Then they followed the candidate inside.

When the door shut, it seemed to cut the questions off dead. For a long moment, there was silence as the reporters finished scribbling their notes or turning off their equipment.

Lansing put her pad in her purse. We turned away. We were about to start down the hill.

"Do you have any comment now, Mr. Wells? Any comment on the congressman's remarks?"

It was Molly. She stuck her microphone at me again. Her cameraman stood behind her, taping me. That thin wicked smile still played on her lips.

"Horseshit," I said. "And you can quote me."

10

I sat at my desk. I pounded at my typewriter. The afternoon had almost become evening now, and I wanted to get my story finished fast. I was writing up my meeting with Mayforth Kendrick. It wasn't exactly what you'd call a scoop, but it was a *Star* exclusive, anyway. It would keep us on top of things for today, at least, if nothing bigger broke.

So I pounded away. I sat in the midst of my papers and trash. I hunched forward over the typewriter. I kept a cigarette clamped between my teeth. I squinted through the smoke at the unrolling page. I pounded away and the noise clattered back and forth off the walls of my cubicle. It rose and spread over the city room.

It was the loudest sound in the joint. All the other typewriters had been replaced by terminal keyboards that barely clacked. The rollicking wire machines had been replaced by computers that booped politely. Most of the loud-mouthed old hacks like me had been replaced by trim, neat, quiet executive-types with advanced degrees in journalism.

Those executive-types would be exchanging glances now. I knew that for a fact. They'd hear the rattle of my Olympia and they'd look at each other and roll their eyes. Wells is writing again, they would mutter. That's what they always muttered and usually I didn't mind. Usually, I figured: They can mutter all they want. They can snicker all the way to the newsstands where they'll see my story on page one again. All that muttering and snickering didn't stop them from coming to me when they needed help on a story. It didn't stop them from speaking my name with a measure of respect. Not usually.

But this time was different. This time, the old machine even sounded noisy to me. It sounded old and out of place. Not up with the times. A dinosaur. Today, when they glanced at each other, those sleek, slick, suited-up postgraduates, I imagined they'd be thinking: *He's slowing down, old Wells. Losing the touch. He's not what he used to be. He's through.*

Or maybe that's just what I was thinking myself.

I was pretty down on old Wells, all right. I'd pretty well had it with him. It's not that I'd been scooped. I'd been scooped before, more times than I wanted to count. It's not that I thought I should have bought Kendrick's photos to beat the competition. The story stank and, as far as I was concerned, the competition could have it.

Hell no: it's not that I'd been scooped on the story. It's that I'd been stuck with it.

Because now I had no options. My reputation was on the line. Bush was calling me an incompetent. Abingdon was calling me a liar or a dupe. Whoever had those pictures wasn't going to step forward waving them in the air like a confession of murder: If I wanted to prove I was telling the truth, if I wanted to prove I could still get at the truth, I was going to have to find them—them or the girl in them. I was going to have to cover this dirty little tale like a blanket.

After twenty-six years in the business, I was about to become everything I hated in the business. I was about to become relatable.

So I pounded away. The pages of the story coiled up out of the Olympia. When each one reached the end, I ripped it out and tossed it amidst the litter on the desk. I tipped the ash off my cigarette. I shot another page into the typewriter. I pounded away.

Then it was done. I packed the pages together. I didn't

reread it. I didn't have the stomach for it. I carried it across
the room to the city desk and dumped it in Rafferty's lap.
He didn't even look down.

"Seeya," he murmured.

I held up my hand to him as I kept walking. I went out
the glass doors, out into the city to find Georgia Stuart.

The sun was gone, but not the heat. The last summer
light was still lingering, and so was the swamp gas that had
passed for air these last few days. By the time I climbed
into the Artful Dodge, I was dragging my sleeve over my
forehead again. I switched on the engine and the air conditioner. I drove off through the gloaming.

I went straight along Forty-second Street, west. West,
past the last liquid mass of commuters flowing toward Grand
Central Terminal. Past the white headlights coming down
Fifth Avenue, and the red taillights pulling away through
the heat. Past the cool, sleepy gazes of the library's stone
lions. Down past Broadway, where the street fans out like
a deck of cards and becomes the towering billboards and
flashing lights of Times Square. And on past that, where
the bright Broadway lights grow sad and stone-faced and
gaudy on the ads for porno shows.

Finally, those lights also fell away. At either window,
there were small restaurants interspersed with small marquees. There were small groups of young people walking
together, talking, gesturing with their hands. There were
strips of neon and strips of darkness. This was Theater Row.

I started at a place called the Walden. It was on the
ground floor of an ancient tower of white brick. I walked
inside, into a cube of a room, and found a girl sitting behind
a sawed-off door. A sign above her said BOX OFFICE. I
flashed my press card at her. She pointed me back through
a curtain.

I came into the auditorium. There were maybe fifty seats
dropping sharply down toward a little stage. On the stage

was a cluttered set that looked like some poor farmer's kitchen. An old fridge, a battered table, a few chairs, a general mess on the countertops. I came down the aisle, climbed up on the stage. One spotlight was on me there. I paused under its light a second. I had the eerie feeling of having stepped through a door into Kansas.

I walked across the kitchen to the front door. I opened it and walked out. I was in a tight space formed by the stage behind me and a curtain in front. I walked through the middle of the curtain. I did not think I was in Kansas anymore.

I had entered a broad dark expanse, hung with wires, littered with stacked chairs. It was crowded with people, loud with their noise. Two young men and two women in leotards were shifting a sofa here and there. Setting it down. Pausing to debate. Shifting it again. Two older men, both bearded, were arguing in each other's faces. A young man walked by with his thumbs hooked in old-fashioned farm suspenders. He looked about twenty, but heavy lines had been painted on his brow and around his mouth.

I stopped him as he passed. I showed him my press card. His back straightened. "What's this for?" He had a deep soft voice that ran along like a stream.

"It's for a story I'm doing."

"On the theater? On the play?"

"On her." I took the Xeroxed photo of Georgia out of my pocket. I unfolded it, held it under his nose.

He stared down at her, his thumbs hooked in his suspender straps. I looked away from him as a pretty young woman in her underwear sort of skipped by me, calling, "Charlie!" The others were moving the couch again.

"Yeah," said the young farm boy. "I've seen her. I've seen her around at auditions. But, you know." He shrugged. "You see everyone there."

"Don't know her name?"

"Nah. Check in the dressing room." He gestured with

his head toward the space behind me. He really did look like a farmer when he did that. He never let his suspenders go.

I thanked him. Wandered away. I skirted the moving sofa, came around a partition. There was a doorway, lighted brightly in the general gloom of the place. I walked through, into a thin room. A corridor nearly. There was a long mirror running the length of one wall. Clothes hanging sloppily from hooks on the other. In the cramped space between were three men, four women and a row of stools. The women all had black tights on. Two wore sweatshirts, one wore a bra. The one just near me was bare-breasted. She was sitting on a stool, leaning toward the mirror, clipping long, purple earrings on her ears. She was chewing gum. She was breathtaking. Two of the guys were in nothing but bikini briefs. The third had overalls on.

I cleared my throat. The actors looked up. The lady with the earrings quietly, unhurriedly, reached for a T-shirt and slipped it over her head.

I told them who I was. None of them seemed to recognize the name. They gathered around me. I showed them the picture. They hovered over it, shouldering each other in the small space.

"Yeah," said one of the guys in briefs. "I've seen her around."

"Another guy was just looking for her," said a different guy in a different pair of briefs. "This gigantic cracker asked me about her."

"Yeah, that's right," said the woman in the bra. "I told him: I've seen her in auditions. I remember her 'cause she was so good."

An attractive middle-aged woman in a sweatshirt smiled sharply. "Was the other guy a reporter too? She's gotta be good to rate all this press."

"He wasn't press, he was a friend," I said. "No one seems to be able to find her, so I thought I'd see if there was a missing person story in it. You know: country girl comes to the big city and vanishes."

The woman with the earrings was close to me. Her shoulder was rubbing mine. She smelled of talcum powder. It made my head light. She snapped her gum.

"Georgia something. Stuart," she said. "We got a callback on an Ibsen play about, I don't know, four months ago. We read together. She was real focused—intense. It was nice stuff. I thought she'd get the part. We talked a little while we waited."

"Did she mention where she was staying?"

Earrings looked up at me. She had a complexion like porcelain. She had rich, pale lips. She had eyes a foggy, purple color. She studied me for a long moment, chewing her gum.

She broke the glance. I felt it snap. "Okay, let me think," she said. She shook her head. "I don't remember anything like that. We just talked the business. Bitched, basically."

The other six actors had moved away. They were bumping into each other as they resumed their stations before the mirror.

"Can you remember anything she said?" I asked.

She moved her head back and forth. The long earrings shivered and flashed in the bright mirror light. "Just the usual. She seemed kind of an innocent. She was from the Midwest somewhere, I remember. She'd sort of come here thinking, well, you know, she was real pretty and such a great actress so she should be able to walk on stage and get a job. Now that she'd been here a couple months, been the rounds, she found out it wasn't so easy. I don't think she'd landed anything. . . . Yeah—that was her first callback; that's what started the conversation. She was talking like, you know, it was unfair. Said she was thinking of taking classes to make some contacts; thinking of going home." She smiled. It lifted her round cheeks. It made her purple eyes bright. "The usual sad story," she said.

I tried to think of something else to ask her. I wanted to hear her speak again. I wanted to keep smelling her powder.

I said, "Her friend, the big guy—he didn't talk to you, I take it."

"Nope. He must have come by when I was out," she said. "Look, I've got to get dressed."

"Oh. Yeah. Sure." I couldn't think of any way to make her stay. I thanked her. I walked away. A little weight of regret settled in my belly. Down there with all the rest of them.

I was encouraged too, though. One theater, my first try, and' I'd found several people who'd known her and one who had actually talked to her. It seemed like a good sign.

It was a deceptive sign, it turned out. As Wally had told me, plenty of people had seen Georgia, plenty had seen her at auditions and the like. But no one seemed to know her or to know where she was. I covered every theater I could find. I walked from marquee to marquee in the night-heat. I went to theaters the size of packing crates and tenth-floor theaters in lost and dusty rooms. I went to elegant places with winding staircases under chandeliers, and one or two spots that were no more than a broad floor and a bunch of benches.

At every theater, I passed around the picture. Yeah, said the actors they'd seen her around. They'd auditioned with her. She was pretty. She was good. She complained about how hard it was to get work. They all complained about how hard it was to get work. Some of them had been questioned by Wally. Some of them he'd missed. None of them had the faintest idea of where Georgia lived, or where she'd ever lived. No one had seen her lately.

Around eight o'clock, I came out of a theater called The Actor's Space. I had finally run out of steam. The shows were beginning up and down the block. I couldn't get backstage to question the actors anymore.

I stood still under the marquee. The night heat was stultifying. The gutter stink was heavy in the air. The exhaust from busses rolling by was enough to suffocate me. I rubbed the back of my neck. I puffed my cheeks and blew. I was hot. I was tired. I was hungry.

Across the street from me was Cole's. It was one of those newfangled restaurants, all windows and wooden tables, with young people leaning toward each other clasping big glasses of wine. A big glass of wine sounded pretty good right now. Almost as good as a big glass of scotch with maybe a steak on the side. I waited for a break in the traffic and headed across Forty-second.

I came into a broad expanse dotted with tables and chairs. At the center of it, on a raised platform, was a long, white bar. There were lots of potted palms by the huge windows. Where the windows gave way to walls, there were bars of neon, red and blue. Under the neon were posters from old Broadway shows. *Fifty Million Frenchmen. Dubarry Was A Lady. Anything Goes.*

I grabbed a table under the bar platform. I called to a waitress. She brought me a scotch. I looked her over. A would-be actress by the looks of her. A knockout. She had a lion's mane of sable hair. She had red, bee-stung lips. She had startling light eyes. She had a perfect shape, full and slim and full again, and it was shown off well by the skirted black leotard she wore.

"Can I take your order?" she said. She had a smooth, velvety voice.

"Yeah," I said. "A steak, medium rare."

"We have chateaubriand."

"Is that anything like a hunk of meat?"

"Only vaguely."

"I'll take a club sandwich and fries."

She was gone. I leaned back. I lit a cigarette. I sipped my drink. The two went well together. I pulled the picture of Georgia Stuart from my pocket. I unfolded it and looked it over.

It was a sweet face. Freckled across the bridge of the little nose. Freckled on the round cheeks. She had a slight

smile on her lips and her lips looked very soft. Her eyes
were kind and quiet. Her hair was light and flowed gently
to her shoulders. I gazed into that face and wondered what
a nice girl like her had been doing in a photo like Kendrick's.
It didn't seem to make a whole lot of sense. But then I
thought about the other girl, the one I'd met tonight in the
dressing room. The one with the purple earrings and no
shirt. She wasn't any older than this kid. Hell, she wasn't
any older than my own daughter would've been if she'd
stayed alive. She probably came here from Wichita or K.C.
or Omaha. Probably thought she was being sophisticated
or sharp, walking around like that. Living alone here, with
no one to take care of her . . .

I heard a noise behind me. A short, sharp intake of breath,
almost a gasp. I turned and saw my waitress. She was carrying my club and fries on a tray, but she had come to a
stop a few feet from the table. She was staring over my
shoulder at the picture in my hand.

The moment I looked at her, she turned it off. Her pretty
face went blank. She took the next step and set down the
tray. She dealt me the club. Her cheek was an inch from
me. I studied it.

"I need to find her," I said.

She didn't answer. She straightened. She glanced at the
bar. Back at me.

"Why? Are you a cop?"

"God, no."

"A private eye?"

"There's no such thing as a private eye. I'm a reporter.
John Wells of the *Star*." The name did nothing for her
either. It seemed actors didn't care much about the day's
news. I said: "She may be involved in a story I'm doing. I
want to find out."

The woman walked away. I cursed. I crushed out my
cigarette. I pulled the club sandwich toward me. The woman
came back. She'd dumped the tray. She sat down in the

chair across from me. She pushed a slip of paper toward me.

"That's her address," she said.

I picked up a quarter of sandwich. I chomped it. I munched it, eyeing the paper. "Have a fry," I said.

"Thanks."

"Anyone else ask you about her lately?"

She shook her head. "No. Why?"

I shrugged. I chomped. I munched. "I could use an exclusive right now."

She shrugged back. "Sure," she said. "It's nothing to me." For the first time, I noticed something hard—steely—in those light eyes.

"How'd you know her?"

She swallowed her fry. My cigarette pack and lighter were lying on the table. She took out a butt, lit it. "We worked together in a place downtown."

"A theater?"

"A restaurant. The Prince Street Café."

I kept chomping, munching. "She work there long?"

"Not long. You know. A couple of months."

"You got to know her pretty well then."

"All right. You know."

"Sure. So? What was she like?"

She considered it. "We weren't friends," she said carefully. Then she added: "We talked sometimes though."

"You didn't like her?"

She blew smoke at me. "I never said that."

"No. You didn't. Silly me."

She smiled. I liked her smile. "I gotta go to work," she said. She stood up.

"Listen. Wait a minute."

She waited.

"Well, what's your name?" I asked.

"Susan Scott. I'm here every night but Monday. Till I get a part." She reached down across me to put out her cigarette. The view was nice. She pulled away. I saw the slip of paper again.

"That's a pretty ritzy address," I said. "How does she rate that?"

Her smile soured. "Go ask her," she said.

I watched her as she walked away. I turned back to my sandwich. I chomped. I munched. I stared into the sweet eyes of Georgia Stuart.

11

She lived in a brownstone on Gramercy Park. An elegant old building in a line of elegant old buildings, all of them peering out on the square of grass and statuary that gives the area its name. That square little park sat snug and exclusive behind its iron fence. The trees behind the fence, and the trees on the sidewalks outside the fence with the rest of us, drooped in the windless heat. The old-fashioned street lamps sent halos into the mist. That heavy mist that wouldn't turn to rain.

The Artful Dodge and I went around the square twice looking for a parking space. Finally found one around the corner, on Irving. I walked back to Gramercy past the tables of outdoor cafés, past couples drinking beers at little tables, past the sound of their laughter.

I went down the row of stoops to the address Susan had given me. I climbed the stairs and entered the vestibule.

I looked for Georgia's name on the mailboxes. It wasn't there. Simon was the name on the box that should have been hers. I pressed the button under the name. No answer. I pressed it again. No answer again.

I walked back outside, back down the steps to the baking sidewalk. Above me, the brownstone's door opened. Georgia stepped into the night.

She was wearing a loose white blouse, a short, dark skirt. She had a carryall slung over her shoulder. She paid no attention to me. She came down the stairs briskly. She passed me without a glance and headed for the corner.

"Georgia," I said.

She stopped, swung around. There was a touch of fear in her eyes but there might be in anyone's accosted in the dark like that. There was no other expression on her clear, open face.

"Do I know you?" she asked.

"No." I showed her my press card. "My name is John Wells. I'm with the *New York Star*."

I watched for a reaction. There was none that I could see. The name seemed to do nothing for her.

"Are you a theater writer?" she asked.

I shook my head. "I want to talk to you about Paul Abingdon."

Again: no reaction. Her face remained a blank. She simply twisted her arm so she could look at the giant watch on her wrist. She lifted a shoulder at me. "Listen. I'm going to be late. No offense. Okay?"

She turned her back on me and was off again. She headed toward Park Avenue and the subways.

I tagged after her. We entered the shadows of some sycamores, walking briskly.

"Look," I said. "I'm under the gun. It would help me out if I could talk to you. Get things straight."

"I really am late," was all she said. "I really do have to go."

We came off the shaded street onto south Park. There are no high-toned apartments on this end of the wide avenue. It's offices and warehouses mostly and they're all empty at night. At night, the street belongs to the hookers. I could see them—women with all the charm and tenderness of rusted iron—standing in the gutters, calling to the cars.

We reached the stairs to the subway. Georgia took hold of the banister. She took one step down.

"What about Wally Shakespeare?" I said. "Does that name mean something to you?"

She stopped. She looked over her shoulder at me. She smiled—sadly, I thought. "Oh gee," she whispered.

It was her first show of feeling. Her features softened. Her eyes grew bigger and more kind. I was captured by those eyes. I felt she revealed herself in them, let me see a little of who she was.

I recognized the type. A country girl who had heard the call of the big city. A kid who'd stared east across the high grass and dreamed of a rhythm as fast as the rhythm inside her. I pegged her as the determined type. Ambitious. But nowhere near as tough as she wanted to appear. I could see the innocence she tried to keep hidden. The gentleness she tried to harden without success. Savvy as she tried to seem, I figured she was still a girl in need of a friend, even a guardian. Otherwise, she'd be ripe prey for predators. Like handsome pols looking for a quick fix of power in her bedroom. Or sharp-headed reporters looking for a story that could ruin her life.

"Lookit," I said, "give me half an hour of your time. Clear things up for me one way or the other."

She hesitated, uncertain. I wanted to warn her to turn around and go. I didn't.

"I really should go to class," she said. But she moved away from the stairs and stood beside me.

I took her arm. She didn't protest. We walked back toward the park.

We went to one of the cafés on Irving. One of those where the couples sat together laughing. We sat together, too, at a little table on the sidewalk. We ordered beers. I lit a cigarette.

Georgia watched me. A slight night breeze stirred her hair. She watched me with her lips pressed together and her hands folded on the table. She seemed to be wondering, worrying: Was I friend or foe?

I wasn't sure myself. I thought of those pictures of her with Abingdon. My guess was that she'd been taken in

somehow, seduced. I felt sorry for her. I felt plenty sorry.
But I needed a story by Monday.

"What kind of class you taking?" I asked her.

"Acting. Movement, really." She tilted her chin de-
fiantly. "I'm an actress."

I nodded. "You know Wally's been looking for you, don't
you?"

She lowered her head. She brought her beer up to her
lips and sipped it. "I know," she murmured. Tossing her
hair back, she looked at me. "Did he send you here?"

"No. We just met up with each other along the way. I'm
acting on my own."

"Because I feel so bad about him . . ." Her lips clamped
shut. It was more than she'd meant to say.

I smoked. I watched her. I could see she wanted to talk.
I waited her out.

"Look," she said suddenly. She couldn't hold back. "Look,
Wally is very special to me. He really is. I don't want to
hurt him. But . . . he doesn't understand!"

I looked sympathetic. I'm good at that. It helps during
interviews.

"I mean, this is what I want, Mr. Wells," she said. "I
want to be an actress. Okay? That's why I came here. To
act. And I know I can. And I'm going to do it, no matter
what anybody says." It was her manifesto. She probably
repeated it to herself before she went to sleep at night. She
gave it a curt nod by way of punctuation.

"It's all right with me," I said.

"But not Wally."

I smiled down into my beer. "You know, you're not at
all like he described you."

A quick, wry laugh broke from her. "I'm not surprised.
What did he say?"

"Well . . ." I held up a hand. "I'll tell you. But don't get
mad at me. Okay?"

She laughed again, more warmly this time. She was beginning to relax a little. "Okay," she said.

"Well, according to Wally, you were sort of a juvenile delinquent type. Wandering around middle America's sin-infested shopping malls until he redeemed you with the word of God."

"Oh cripes!" Her eyes went heavenward.

"I didn't say it, remember."

"But don't you see? That's just the thing about Wally. Everything is all right or all wrong with him. All good or all bad. I mean, my friends and I hung around the mall. What else was there to do?" Her hands went up and down. "God, I mean, it's not like we robbed banks or anything."

"I believe you. Really."

She groaned comically. She shook her head. But then she paused, smiled to herself. A fond smile. "When he first came into the mall? To the burger shop? He was so funny. So grim and preachy. We laughed and laughed." She glanced up at me shyly. "Some of the kids were really mean. I felt so sorry for him. I went over to talk to him more because of that than anything. Feeling sorry for him, I mean." She sighed. "Now, I can't get rid of him, Mr. Wells. Do you know I had to move to get away from him."

"You moved to a pretty nice place," I said.

"I was lucky. A friend of mine went on vacation to London. I took his place. I was hoping by the time he came back, Wally would give up and go home."

I smoked my cigarette, considered my timing. I decided to take a crack at it. "I don't think he's going to do that, Miss Stuart. He's pretty worried about this Paul Abingdon thing."

There was a reaction this time. Her mouth turned down. Her eyes grew damp. She considered me closely—accusingly, I thought. "Are you sure you're a reporter?" she asked. Her voice trembled.

"Yeah. More or less," I said. "Why?"

She looked down, hid her face. "I guess I was just hoping . . ." she murmured: "You don't look like a reporter, that's all."

"You know many reporters?"

Her hair went back and forth as she shook her head. She laughed a little. "No." She raised her face again. She had beaten back the tears. "But you're not what I would imagine. I mean, you don't have a reporter's eyes."

I smiled. She smiled back. "What kind of eyes have I got?" I asked her.

And, very serious, she said: "My father's. You have my father's eyes."

I stopped smiling. "No," I said. "Just an old man's eyes, that's all."

"No. Uh-uh. Something else. You have kids, don't you? A daughter, I'll bet."

I didn't answer her. I rolled the tip of my cigarette against the ashtray.

"Don't you?" she said, teasing.

I made a vague gesture.

"Come on. I told you things. You have to tell."

I watched her. "Yeah," I said. "I had a daughter once."

"What do you mean?"

"I mean I had a daughter once. Yeah."

"Oh!" she said. Her lips parted. She actually blushed. The color rose into those round cheeks of hers. Pity rose into those pale eyes. "You mean she . . . Gosh, I'm sorry."

"It's okay. It was a long time ago."

"I'm so sorry. I . . . Was she real sick?"

"No. Not like that, anyway. She killed herself."

"Oh gosh. Oh gosh," said Georgia Stuart.

I didn't answer. I drank in the expression on her face. It was softer than any I'd seen in a while. More gentle. More real. I watched that expression, and I thought about Bush. I thought about Cambridge. I thought about this dirty little story.

"Listen," I said. "Never mind my eyes. I'm a reporter, all right. I'm here for a story. I'm the guy who saw the pictures of you and Abingdon."

She looked away from me. "I don't understand. I don't know what you mean."

"Come on, Georgia. It's been on the radio all day. You know who I am."

Her eyes glistened as the tears returned. "I don't . . . I mean you must have me mixed up with someone else."

"You're a lousy liar," I said. "It was you."

She tightened her lips to stop their trembling. Her hand moved up to her eyes, then fell away. "Well, what about you?" Her voice was pinched and hoarse. "What about what you're doing. What you're trying to do? It's not very nice either, is it? It's not very nice at all."

Her carryall was hung on the back of her chair. She unhooked it, looped the rope of it over her shoulder.

"Excuse me," she said, very softly.

She stood up. I stood up with her. I dumped some cash on the table. The couples in the café around us laughed and talked. Georgia hesitated another second. Then she was weaving through the tables to the sidewalk.

I followed her again. "Look," I said, "there's a murder involved here."

She glanced over at me harshly, but kept walking.

"The cops'll find you eventually. Other papers. You're gonna have to talk to someone."

We'd reached the corner of Gramercy Park South. The trees hovered above us. The shadows hulked around us. The air was so still it seemed to rumble and quake every time a car went by.

Georgia stopped and faced me. Still fighting back the tears, she said: "If I talk to them, will they hurt me any more than you will?"

"I can tell your side . . ." I began to say. Then I stopped. It was every reporter's pitch. The last angle when a source wouldn't crack. I looked down at the sidewalk. I felt like a bum.

When I looked up again, she was walking away from me.

She moved toward her brownstone down the block. I jammed my hands in my pocket. I cursed myself.

A car's engine roared behind me. I spun to the sound. A pair of headlights flashed on. A long black car shot away from the curb with a screech of tires. It sped toward me.

The car whipped by. I saw the silhouette of the man behind the wheel. I saw Georgia glance over her shoulder at it as it came on.

The car slammed to a stop right next to her. A man jumped out of the back. A big man in dark clothing. In an instant, he'd thrown his arm around Georgia's throat.

"Hey!" I shouted. I stepped forward.

One step. By the time I'd taken that one step, the man had dragged Georgia half way into the car. She hadn't even had time to cry out. I saw her legs kicking wildly for a second. Then she was dragged all the way inside.

The car was rolling again before the rear door shut. It sped into the darkness.

I didn't wait to watch it go. I started running toward the Artful Dodge.

12

reached the car in a moment. I tried to jam the keys in
the slot. I couldn't get it. I was losing her. Every second, I
was losing her. The key went in. The door lock popped. I
yanked the door open, jumped inside.

It was suffocating in there. The air had turned to stone. I
got the key in the ignition, hit the pedal, pumped the old
jalopy to life. I wrenched the wheel over and tried to pull
out. Nearly clipped a van as it passed. I was jolted forward
as I slammed on the brakes. Losing her. Losing her.

Finally, I pulled out into the street. I barreled toward
the corner. I had to pull around the van. I heard its brakes
scream as it stopped to avoid broadsiding me. I heard its
driver scream as I swung in front of him. I sped away down
Gramercy. I peered through the windshield, searching for
the dark car.

I saw a pair of taillights up ahead a block. I hit the gas. I
was panting, sweating. Clumsily, I rolled down the window
with my left hand, steering with my right. The breeze
swept in. It was a hot breeze, but better than nothing.

The light on Third Avenue was green. The car ahead of
me bounced through the intersection. I caught a glimpse
of it for a moment under the lights of the avenue. It was
the dark car. I rushed after it.

The light turned yellow. The broken line of cars on the
avenue prepared to go. The dark car pulled away down the
other side of Twentieth. I crushed the pedal under my sole.

The Artful Dodge rocketed beneath the light as it turne
red, plunged into the darkness on the other side.

I ran fast between two lines of parked cars. Brownston
went by in a blur on either side of me. Then—suddenly—
the red taillights ahead of me were growing bigger. Close
The dark car had stopped short. I was nearly on top of i

I hit the brakes. My tires locked. The Artful Dodge glide
closer and closer to the rear fender of the dark car. I trie
to turn the wheel. The angle of the old Dart shifted. I h
the dark car a glancing blow. Its left taillight exploded in
shower of red shards.

I was thrown forward. My head hit the wheel. I wer
back against the seat hard. I felt blood on my brow. I trie
to clear my head. I hadn't the faintest idea of what the he
was going on.

Vaguely, I noticed the sound of a car door closing.
peered forward. A large man had gotten out of the car
front of me. He was heading back toward me.

"Uuh," I said. I reached forward for the car's controls.
knew I was supposed to do something, but I couldn't qui
figure out what. At last, my hand found the gear shift.
wriggled the metal lever. I pushed the car into reverse.

But by then, the man was standing at the window rigl
next to me. Without thinking, I threw up my arm. Som
thing hit me on the wrist. I fell to one side, groaning wit
the pain.

The thug at the window reached in. He groped for th
door lock. I watched him, dazed. He found the lock. H
grabbed it.

I rolled up to a sitting position, bringing my fist aroun
in an arc as I came. The fist hammered the back of th
thug's hand.

I heard him grunt. He pulled his hand away. He cam
at me again—with a sap, that's what he had, a little blac
jack. He flicked it at my face. It glanced off my left eyebrov
driving me back from the window again.

This time, he reached in all the way and grabbed th

inside door handle. I got a look at his face. It was hairless, with skin a dull silver color, like fish scales. It had a harelip, as if the whole lower part had been smeared before it had a chance to dry. The eyes stared at me crazily as he pulled up on the handle.

The latch snapped. The thug pulled out of the window, drew back the door. He rumbled toward me like an avalanche, grabbed me by the front of the shirt with both hands. He tried to drag me out. I reached up wildly and took hold of his collar. I held on. Then I stepped on the gas.

The car lurched backward. The thug's foul face went wide with surprise as he was yanked off his feet. I held on, steering with my right hand while I gripped him in my left. The thug's feet kicked at the pavement wildly as I dragged him backward.

There was a dull thud. The Dart's rear end had smacked into a parked Porsche. I was thrown forward again and the thug's collar slipped from my grasp. I heard him scream. I saw him fall to the pavement. He rolled across Twentieth Street. He lay still.

Tires screeched. One short sound. The driver of the dark car wasn't waiting around for his muscle man. The red taillights pulled away from me again. They went speeding toward the corner of Second Avenue.

I pulled the door shut and hit the gas in the same moment. I went flying down the street after the dark car.

My head hurt. Blood and sweat ran down the side of my face. My arm felt like the wrong end of a dentist's drill. My heart was beating too damned hard. My lungs were aching.

I kept driving, but now I eased off the gas. I let the dark car stay ahead of me. I let it turn downtown on Second. I let it pull around the corner out of sight. The light was red when I reached the intersection. I edged into the traffic, trying to lose myself. Maybe they'd think I'd been scared off. It was worth trying, anyway.

The dark car sped down Second. Into the lowlands where

the jazz bars sat, and men stood drinking under the darkened marquees of used-up theaters. I followed, keeping my distance. Weaving back and forth amid the other cars, staying lost, staying down. Into the glare of the East Village. The newsstands and delis and restaurants too brightly lit. Down, finally, into the Bowery with its high walls of faceless buildings lowering above streets abandoned to the night. Empty except for the white litter strewn from gutter to gutter. Lifeless except for the bodies of bums stretched out on the sidewalk.

The traffic began to fall away. I dropped back a bit more. The dark car slowed, eased over to the left curb, came to a stop.

I stopped, too, half a block back, on the right-hand side. I killed my headlights, my engine. We were on a broad stretch of Bowery. A wide expanse of litter-dotted black tar. There was hardly any traffic at all here, just a wide darkness before me in which nothing seemed to move.

The dark car idled in the shadow of a squat building. It was an old place with ornate carvings in the concrete ledges around the big unlit windows.

The door of the dark car opened. A man got out of the passenger side and opened the back door.

Georgia Stuart came out onto the sidewalk. She came out fast, stumbling, as if she'd been pushed. The man on the sidewalk took her roughly by the arm. Another man followed her out of the back seat, unraveling through the door until he stood behind her. The three moved together to the building. As they went through the front door, the dark car sped off behind them.

I got out of the Dodge and crossed the empty street. My footsteps sounded hollow on the pavement as I went quickly to the building.

I peered in through the glass doors. The lobby was small, thin and empty. Almost a corridor, with two elevators in the left wall and a heavy metal door in the back. I slipped inside and moved to the elevators. Their silver doors showed me a blurred reflection. Above the doors were bands of numbers. The band to the left blinked as a lighted six went dark and a dark seven lighted.

The idea of riding up to the seventh floor and stepping out into a round of gunfire didn't appeal to me. I went to the back door instead.

I pulled it open, and stepped through it into a concrete stairwell. The door shut behind me and the lobby light was gone. Up on the first floor landing, though, a red bulb was burning. It sent down a scarlet glow that drew long shadows from everything around.

I started slowly up the stairs. I kept pressed to the wall, trying to see around the landing corner. I came onto the landing and stood under the red bulb. It shone at me from just above the door, just above my head. It lit up a sign on the door which read: REENTRY ON THIS FLOOR. I started climbing again through the mingled scarlet and shadow. On the fifth floor, I stopped for a moment. I peered up the stairs. There was no light on the sixth-floor landing. There was no scarlet glow. There was only blackness.

I took hold of the banister. I climbed. I was breathing hard by now. The sweat had started again. I was covered in it. I went a step and waited, listening. There was silence up there. Up there in the dark. I took another step, listened some more, heard some more silence. I went on, step by step into the shadows.

And then I paused again. And then I heard it.

From beneath me. From the ground floor, it seemed. I heard the door open down there. I heard it swing shut. Then I heard footsteps, climbing the stairs. Slow at first. Then getting quicker. They reached the first floor. They kept coming, quicker still. I listened, breathing hard, covered with sweat. The footsteps came up the stairs faster and faster.

Coming after me.

13

I started my ascent again, but I wasn't moving slowly anymore. I climbed quickly into the darkness above. I swung around the bend, glad to see the red light on the seventh floor landing above me. The footsteps below kept coming, swift and sure. They were maybe two floors below me now.

I hauled my weary bones up the stairs as fast as I could. I was puffing like a bellows, smoking old cigarettes from the inside out.

Then, finally, I was on the seventh floor. I was standing bathed in the red glow, exposed by it. I lunged for the door. I grabbed the knob and pulled. Even before I felt the lock pull back, I saw the sign, two inches from my nose. NO REENTRY ON THIS FLOOR.

The footsteps came on. They were halfway to the dark sixth-floor landing. Three quarters. I shielded my eyes with my left arm. With my right fist, I threw a roundhouse at the light bulb above the door.

There was a sound like a cork coming out of champagne. The bulb imploded, dissolving into a rain of red glass. The filament flared like a torch for a second. Then the blackness closed in on it.

The footsteps stopped. I stood still. I felt the blood start from the knuckles on my right hand. I listened. Under the sound of my own breathing came other breathing from the floor below.

And another sound. The footsteps began again. Slowly,

tentatively. They took the last steps to the sixth-floor landing.

I couldn't just stand there. The landing was small. I had no place to dodge him. If he was armed, I'd be a target even in the dark. I crouched. I started creeping down the stairs.

When I got about halfway down, the faintest outglow of the red bulb on the next floor—the fifth floor—reached me. I saw the sixth landing in a black-red light, like some neglected corner of hell. Into that light came an immense shadow in the shape of a man.

He came suddenly, swinging around the corner as if he expected an ambush. He was armed, all right. He was raising his gun at the landing where I had just been.

I threw myself down the stairs at him. Hit him hard, right in the midsection. I jammed my left arm up against his right, hoping to deflect the fire of the gun. But the gun didn't go off. As I grappled with the shadow in the darkness, I saw the weapon spinning into the red light of the next landing down. The gun hit the wall, dropped to the stairs. It bounced onto the concrete floor and slid across it with a loud clatter.

Me and my shadow did battle on the landing above. We grabbed each other, slapped and clawed, seeking out pressure points we couldn't see. My right wrist was locked in his left hand. His fingers tried to tear at my cheek. My thumb tried to find his eye to gouge it. I pressed forward, my teeth bared, hoping to take a bite of him. We wrestled in an eerie quiet of grunts and gasps.

Then he broke free and went after the gun.

He ripped himself from my grasp, threw himself to the side. He went over the edge of the landing, half ran, half stumbled down the stairs as I scrabbled for purchase on his clothes or his flesh. Then I was all over him and, locked together, we went down. We hit the concrete with a force that shook my bones, jarred the wind from me. We slid and bounced down the stairs, clubbing at each other all the way.

Once again we were in the weird scarlet world the light made. The black shadows of it flared and wavered all around us as we struggled to reach the gun in the corner. My lungs burned. My stomach rolled. He was scratching me, slapping at me, pounding at my head. I kept swinging my fist wherever his face was. Now he got in a short, sharp shot to my abdomen. Already breathless, I grunted and doubled up. The thug rolled over onto his belly. He threw out his hand toward the weapon.

I straightened and vaulted over him. I landed lengthwise on top of him, my hand outreaching his by an inch, maybe two. I wrapped my fingers around the warm plastic of the gun's grip. The thug pulled himself out from under me, but now I had a firm hold on the gun.

That's when he stuck another gun into my ear.

"Drop it, fuckhead," he gasped.

I groaned. I released the gun I'd grabbed. I rolled away and sat up against the wall, hacking, gagging. I thought I was going to throw up.

The thug had gotten to his knees. He had a revolver leveled at my head. He was wheezing so hard he sounded like he was crying out in pain with every breath. After a second, he managed to get one foot under him, then the other. He stood over me. I coughed thick phlegm into my mouth as I wondered if he was going to pull the trigger and blow my head apart.

The barrel of the pistol jerked in the scarlet light. "Get up, fuckface," the thug said, gasping.

It wasn't easy. I rolled over onto my hands and knees first. I coughed and gasped. I pushed my hands against the concrete and dragged one foot under me. I coughed some more. I gasped some more. I seemed to be bleeding everywhere. I dragged the other foot under me. I took hold of the wall. I pulled myself up.

I faced him. It was the harelip, the guy who'd come at
‹ in my car. He pointed the gun at my belly.

"I thought I dropped you," I said.

"I got up," he said.

"I thought I beat you here," I said.

"I took a cab," he said.

I looked down at the gun in his hand. I looked over at
‹ gun in the corner, an automatic.

"I thought I had your gun at least," I said.

"What, that old thing," he said. "I only wear that when
‹ot nothing to wear."

He whipped the pistol around in an arc. It slapped into
‹ side of my head. I fell to my knees again. I pitched
‹ward onto my face.

It had hardly been worth the effort of standing.

14

"Where are the pictures, Georgia?" Quietly, almost gent
"I don't . . . I don't . . ." She was crying.
There was a slap. A scream.
"Where are the pictures, Georgia?"
"I don't . . ."
A slap again. Another scream. Sobbing.
His gentle voice: "This is going to get much, much wor
lady."
Sobbing and sobbing.
I heard it all before I saw it, before I saw it proper
took it in. It seemed to repeat and repeat without endir
"Now: Where are the pictures, Georgia?"
"I don't . . ."
The blow, the scream, the sobs.
I wrenched my eyes open. I was lying in a corner o
room. A small office. It was brightly lit. It seemed brigh
lit to me, anyway. To me, it seemed to be sitting in t
center of the sun. I shut my eyes again. The words, t
sound of blows, the sobs continued. I forced my eyes ope
I squinted into the blinding light.

I saw Georgia. They had her in a chair. An armless swi
chair. She looked very small huddled in it. Her hands we
in her lap. Her chin was on her chest. Her shoulders sho
with sobbing. I could see the tears running down one
her cheeks. The cheek was purple.

A man in a navy suit was sitting on the edge of a desk
front of her. I could see his profile. It was not a very ni

profile. It was long and elegant enough. His hair was slicked
back and tidy. But all the features were sharp and cruel.
His eyes peered down from the desk at the weeping girl
and there was nothing in those eyes except maybe the gleam
of pleasure. I knew the man. It was Alphonse Marino.

Right behind Georgia stood a monster. He must have
been six foot six, at least. Across. God knows how tall he
was. He had a square head like the Frankenstein monster
with a face as pretty. At a gesture from Marino, he grabbed
a handful of Georgia's light brown hair. He yanked her
head up.

"Where are the pictures, Georgia?" Marino said gently.

She stared at him. She looked scared. Plenty scared.
Scared enough to give him anything he wanted, anything
she had. But all she did was shake her head. I could see
the monster's grip tightening on her hair.

"Please," she said.

Marino's hand shot out. The back of it raked her purple
cheek. Her lip opened now. A thin stream of blood dribbled
down over her chin. The monster let go of her hair. Her
head fell forward. Her shoulders shook. She sobbed.

I saw another movement, turned my head. The hare-
lipped thug was leaning against the opposite wall. He looked
like I felt. His cheeks were scratched up. His neck was
bruised. There was a mouse around his right eye that was
bigger than Mickey. All the same, he was gazing down at
Georgia and his disfigured lip was lifted in a derisive smile.
He snorted at her as she sobbed.

Marino stared at Georgia coldly. He began to gesture
toward Frankenstein again. I groaned. His eyes shifted to
me. I pushed myself into a sitting position. I leaned against
the wall. I tried to smile. It hurt. I smiled anyway.

Marino sneered at me. He'd loved me never. I'd made
some trouble for him in my time. Did an exposé that scotched
a construction bid he had an interest in. Wrote a piece that
kept his brother from a political chairmanship. Probably the
one that bugged him most was the story I did on Palooka-

ville, a horse he owned. Got her disqualified from the Preakness for drug use.

He had the Artful Dodge's tires slashed for that one, broke her windshield, dented her doors. That was as close to a confrontation as he and I had ever come. His boss—Dellacroce—did not like making war on the press.

So anyway, he sneered at me. And I just kept smiling. I said: "Well, if it isn't Alphonse Marino beating up on a helpless woman."

He lifted one perfect eyebrow. I wondered if he'd had it clipped. "Well," he said softly, "if it isn't John Wells lying on the floor like a piece of shit."

"Why, Alphonse, I do believe you're offering me a chair in your own slimy way."

I got my feet under me and pushed my way up the wall. Harelip straightened as I made the move, but a glance from Marino kept him calm. I took a stumbling step and dropped down into a chair beside the desk.

I gestured weakly toward Georgia. She went in and out of focus. She sobbed and sobbed.

"I like this," I said, gesturing at her. "Politics Dellacroce style. Innovative."

Marino's eyes seemed veiled like a snake's eyes. "Shut up," he said sweetly.

"How did you find her anyway?"

He sneered some more. "We followed you right to her," he said. "Sure. We heard your name on the radio and just tagged right after you. Thanks, Wells."

Georgia sobbed. I studied Marino. He wasn't making sense, but my head was too rattled to figure it out. "That's very smart," I said slowly. "That's positively brainy."

"Thanks," he said again, "now shut the fuck up before I kick your teeth down your throat."

I nodded. But I did not shut up. I kept talking, stalling. "So this is Maldonado's campaign strategy. You beat her up, get the pictures. Abingdon withdraws. Maldonado becomes senator. Very nice."

"Now, now, now," he warned me gently. "Don't forget those teeth."

"Mr. Maldonado goes to Washington. Downright patriotic."

This time, Marino smiled with both sides of his mouth. "You're going to be dead soon, Wells," he said.

"After you, Alphonse."

He stopped smiling. He considered me. I got the feeling he was measuring me for a shroud.

After a moment, he reached inside his navy blue jacket. He pulled out a gold cigarette case and popped it open. He took out a long smoke with a gold band under the filter. He laid it gently in his mouth. He lit it tenderly with a golden lighter.

He turned back to Georgia.

As he put the case and the lighter back in his jacket, he gestured at Frankenstein with his chin. This time, as the monster grabbed hold of Georgia's hair with one hand, he caught hold of the front of her blouse with the other. He ripped the cloth with one swift, brutal movement. She screamed and bucked forward in the chair. He tore the blouse away, exposing her bra.

"Please," she managed to say.

He tore the bra off with a swipe of his big hands.

Marino pulled on his fancy cigarette. He made the tip of it glow. He pulled it from his mouth and studied the glowing tip.

"Oh God please," Georgia said. She crossed her hands desperately over her breasts. "I don't have it, I don't have it, I swear to God, I never had them, never, never, I don't know where they are, I swear I swear . . ." She kept on babbling while Marino turned the cigarette in his hand, studying this angle of the tip and that one. Then he laid it down carefully in an ashtray that sat on the corner of the desk between us.

"You have pretty tits," he said.

"Oh please, oh God," said Georgia.

"In thirty seconds I'm going to burn out the centers of them."

Hairlip chuckled at his place against the wall.

"First one of them," said Marino, "then the other."

Georgia's mouth moved. Saliva clung to the lips. Tears poured down her cheeks. No words came out anymore.

"For Christ's sake, Marino," I said.

"Shut up, Wells," he said dreamily.

"Look at her, for Christ's sake. If she had the pictures, she'd tell you. Look at her."

He was looking at her. He gazed on her lovingly as she shook and covered herself and cried. A faint smile played at the corner of his mouth. He was dreaming of how it would be.

"Twenty seconds," he said. He was hoarse now. "Where are the pictures, Georgia?"

"I don't . . ." Georgia managed.

"Marino, you bastard . . ." I said.

"He said shut up," said the Harelip. He didn't even look at me. He, too, was staring at the girl.

Marino waited, watching. "Fifteen seconds," he said. "Where are the pictures?"

Georgia cried and cried.

"Ten," said Marino. Without removing his gaze from the girl, he reached for the cigarette. His fingers touched the ashtray. They felt around the edges. They didn't find the butt. Marino glanced down. He saw the ashtray was empty. He glanced up, at me.

I blew a lungful of smoke at him.

"My brand, too," I said.

He smiled down at me. It was a look of wonder. He chuckled. "That cigarette is going to be very bad for your health," he said.

"Fuck you, Marino." I crushed the cigarette out. He watched me do it. I stood up. Harelip came off the wall. I didn't even look at him. I planted myself in front of Marino with my back to Frankenstein and Georgia. I pointed a finger at the thug's chest. "I've had enough of this shit," I said. "You're not burning anyone. The fun's over." I lowered the finger I was pointing and put the hand in my pocket. I didn't want him to see how badly it was shaking. My voice was shaking, too. I had to talk fast to cover it. "Your jackass kicked me around pretty good tonight, but I'm going to overlook that because I'm a nice guy. I'm afraid I have to be a little bit more severe about the girl. You can't slap her anymore, and burning her with cigarettes is strictly taboo. If you do, I'll just have to report the matter to the newspaper-reading public."

Marino just stared at me. He could not speak. I pushed on.

"And when I report it, Mr. Marino, you know what that means? It means Maldonado has no more chance of making it to the U.S. Senate than Palookaville has of winning the Triple Crown. And should that become the case, a certain Mr. Dellacroce, believed in law enforcement circles to be the leading luminary of the Dellacroce crime family, is going to be very, very perturbed. Somebody's going to pay for it, pal, and it won't be me."

Marino's cruel lips parted. I was rolling again before he got a word in.

"Oh sure," I said. "I know what you're thinking." I almost took my hand out of my pocket, but the minute it released its death grip on the flannel, it began quaking like Los Angeles on a bad day. I grabbed hold again and kept it there. "You're thinking: Well, hell, if I just kill this guy, then I won't have to worry about his writing this sordid little story on the front page for all to see. But you're wrong there, Marino. You're dead wrong. And I'll tell you why you're dead wrong. Sure I will." I felt almost certain there was a reason. I just had to come up with it. I said: "Sure I'll tell you why you're dead wrong. You're dead wrong because if you kill me, every reporter in this town'll be after you and in a couple of other towns besides. They won't need to get all the facts either. Even their worst guesses

will put an end to Maldonado's Senate bid. Sure. So just
let the girl go, pal, and maybe I'll be good to you and forget
the whole thing."

"Kill him," Marino said.

Harelip pulled out his automatic. Marino glanced at him.
"Do it in the stairwell," he said.

Hairlip stepped across the room. He lifted the automatic
and placed the bore to my forehead. It felt cold.

"Let's go out to the stairwell," he said.

"Good-bye, Wells," said Marino.

I turned around and started for the door. As I stepped
out of the office, I heard a clicking noise and glanced back.
Marino had taken out his gold cigarette case again. He was
looking at Georgia again. She was staring after me in wide-
eyed horror. Then her attention was drawn away by the
voice of Marino.

"Now," he murmured, "as I was saying . . ."

15

Harelip was good. He knew what he was doing. He stayed right behind me with the fingers of his left hand pressed lightly between my shoulder blades. The other hand, the hand with the gun in it, he kept back, close to his body. That way, he could march me along briskly, but keep me from swinging around and knocking the weapon loose.

We came out of the office into a dark reception area. Harelip hurried me through. We turned a corner. We came to a wooden door. I tried reaching for the knob.

"Ey!" said Harelip. I dropped my hand to my side.

Now, he placed the barrel of the gun firmly in the small of my back. His left hand came around me and pulled the door open. With the gun pressed tight against me and his left arm surrounding me, I couldn't turn or move quickly. I couldn't get any leverage on him. He shoved me through the door.

We entered the foyer, where the elevators were. A ceiling fluorescent fluttered dully, lighting about fifteen yards of floor. Dirty linoleum, big black-and-white squares like a checkerboard. At the other end of those fifteen yards was the heavy metal door that led to the stairwell. I looked at it, and my breathing got short. A bolt of electric fear went through me. It did not seem very far to that door at all. It didn't seem like there was much time to think of a way out of this. It didn't seem like there was a way out of this. Nothing to do but march quietly to my place of execution.

We started walking toward the door.

I tried to break his concentration. Get him talking.

"Let me ask you something," I said. My voice was high and breathy: I was that afraid.

Harelip said nothing. He marched me forward, step by step.

"How did you guys really find the girl? You couldn't have followed me. You couldn't have known I'd look for her."

Harelip said nothing. We were ten yards from the door. I began to imagine my body on the other side of it—as if we'd open the door and find it lying there.

"Maybe it was Kendrick. Maybe he told you before you killed him," I said. "Sure. Marino took him out for pimping in his territory, and Kendrick tried to buy him off with the pictures. But then you'd have the photos already, wouldn't you?"

Harelip said nothing. Step by step. Five yards.

"But it was Kendrick, wasn't it?" I said. "He had a big mouth. Hung out in your circles. He must have just spread the word around too far."

Harelip said nothing. He kept his fingers to my back, he kept the gun to his body, out of my reach. He marched me across the last yards to the stairwell door.

Once again, he planted the automatic in my kidney. He reached around me and grasped the knob. It was the same move he'd made before, as we came into the foyer. Only this time, I knew it was coming. This time, as he moved, I moved too.

It was that one second when he shifted his balance. I figured I had time for one motion then. I reached across myself with my right hand and grabbed his outstretched wrist while, at the same instant, I shot my left elbow back, knocking his gun hand wide.

I kept coming around until I was facing him. Then I let go of his wrist and jabbed my fingers into his eye.

I hit him solid. I felt the aspic of the eyeball give under my fingertips. Harelip gave one short, choked, high-pitched shriek. He fell back from me with one hand to his face as the other waved the automatic wildly in the air. I stepped forward and drove my fist hard into his gut.

This time, his scream was deep and it came from deep in his throat. He deflated, slowly, bending forward, sinking down. The automatic dropped to the floor. So did the gunman.

I stooped and recovered the automatic. I went inside Harelip's coat and got the revolver, too. I straightened up. Harelip lay on his side, clutching his belly. He was staring straight ahead, right at my ankles. He was staring kind of stupidly, but he was still conscious. I didn't like that. I kicked him in the face.

That put his lights out. He rolled over from the force of the blow. His eyelids stayed up but only white was showing in there now.

I looked down at the gun in my hand. I'm not very good with guns. I don't need them much in my line of work and frankly they scare the bejesus out of me. But it would have been easy just then to point this one at the bleeding thug and pull the trigger. At least, I thought it would be easy.

But I didn't try it. I turned away from him and started back across the foyer. I went quickly, the gun out in front of me, through the door, through the reception area, back to the office where Georgia was. I pushed the door in and went in after it.

I had a moment, before they reacted, to catch the tableau. The monster-man was still in back of Georgia. He had his hand cupped under her chin and was dragging her head backward. He had both her hands behind her back and was keeping them pinned there, with both her wrists gripped tight in one of his paws. So he had the front of her completely exposed to Marino. And Marino was stepping forward with that cigarette of his.

I pointed the automatic at the monster's kneecap. My hand shook badly. I'd never shot anyone before. It isn't easy, it turns out.

But I pulled the trigger. The gun jolted in my hand. A

wind seemed to blow the side of the monster's trousers up around his thigh. The next thing I knew, he was letting out a kind of gurgling roar and falling to the ground with a thud that made the whole room shake.

I turned the gun on Marino.

"And I'm not even angry yet," I said.

He seemed convinced. He put his hands up in the air just like in the movies. He didn't say a word. He just watched as I walked over to Georgia, grabbed her by the upper arm and lifted her out of the chair.

I pulled her close to my side. I glanced down at Frankenstein. He was still writhing and grimacing in his pain. But now his hand had started moving toward his jacket.

I kept the gun on Marino.

"He's not quick enough," I lied.

Marino glanced at the monster nervously. "Okay. Forget it," he said.

The monster let his hand return to his shattered leg. His pants were covered with blood now. He lay on the floor, grunting. He pointed that big square head of his straight at me. He stared at me dully with his enormous eyes. I got the distinct impression he was memorizing my face.

I backed toward the door, taking Georgia with me. She was still making small noises deep in her throat. She was staring around like a frightened animal. I'm not even sure she knew where she was.

I kept moving until my back touched the door. I stopped and looked Marino in the eye. He smiled at me.

Softly, he said: "How long do you think . . . ?"

"Shut up," I said. There was no way to hide the shaking in my voice now. "Shut up and listen, you piece of shit. I'm taking the lady and getting out of here. If you want me, I'll be at the *Star*. I'll be at my desk writing all this down, everything I saw here tonight. It ought to be in Saturday's editions. Front page. So if anything happens to the girl, you'll be the first one they'll come for. Count on that, Marino. Because I'll make sure of it."

He didn't answer. He seemed to be thinking. Maybe he was thinking about Dellacroce reading Saturday's paper. Or about Dellacroce losing his Senate candidate. Or about Alphonse Marino losing his job, the mobster way.

I let go of Georgia. She swayed for a moment so that I thought she'd go over. Then she steadied herself. I reached back and got the doorknob. I edged the door open and gestured her out with my head.

I faced Marino one last time. "Remember, Alphonse, anything happens to her, the *Star*'ll hang you." I started backing out the door. "Anything happens to me," I said, "and there'll be a nasty little editorial besides."

And I was out of there.

16

Harelip was starting to stir when we came out into the foyer. I kept an eye on him as we waited for the elevator. I kept one hand on the girl and one hand on the gun until we were inside the box, and the doors had slid closed.

Then I let Georgia go. She stood in the corner, her face pressed against the elevator's cold metal. She was hugging her shoulders, her arms crossed over her naked breasts. She did not make a noise.

I leaned back against the wall. My sore, bleeding face broke into a sweat all over. I stared at the doors in front of me. My mouth hung open. I breathed through it. I kept thinking about the cracking sound the gun had made when I'd fired it. I kept seeing the wind blow Frankenstein's trousers. I kept feeling the jolt of the automatic in my hand. It wasn't pleasant. I began to feel nauseous.

The elevator went down. I rolled my head to look at Georgia in the corner. She continued to cower there.

"Well," I said, "that's the power of the press for you."

I heard her make a noise. A laugh, it sounded like. That seemed to bust the dam. She hit the wall with her fist and cried out, "Oh!" Then she started sobbing. The sound was very loud and full of anguish. She hit the wall with her fist again and again as she sobbed.

The elevator touched down. I tensed, waiting for the door to open. Maybe some of them were out there. Maybe they were waiting for us, just standing out there with their guns already aimed at the door. Georgia just kept pound

ng the wall. She used her open palm now. She kept
sobbing.

The doors opened. There was no one out there. Georgia
kept slapping the wall and sobbing.

"Come on," I said.

I took her by the arm. I drew her to me. I put my arm
around her shoulders. Her flesh felt warm under my palm.
Her breasts felt soft against my side.

I kept the automatic in front of me. I followed it out of
the elevator, across the lobby, through the front doors, into
the night. The heat was still out there. It was dangling there,
sodden, like a wet blanket on a laundry line. When I looked
up and down the street, I could see the haze of it. The
shimmer in the lamplight, the halo of humidity. I was already covered with sweat, but I started sweating all over
again as we crossed the broad avenue. I kept looking left
and right at the deserted pavement. White litter motionless
on the blacktop. The midtown skyline rising up at the end
of a corridor of stone.

Georgia kept sobbing. She was still sobbing when I put
her in the car. When I walked around to the driver's side,
I had to let myself in. She just sat there with her arms
crossed in front of her, with her chin on her chest, sobbing.

I got in. I turned on the ignition, the lights. I flipped it
into gear.

Georgia swung around to me. Her hair lashed her face
as she turned. Her cheeks were blotchy, her mouth was
twisted, her eyes were hot. "Those . . . bastards!" she cried.
"Those *bastards!*"

I pulled away from the curb. I swung the car around. I
tore up the avenue. I did not stop at the lights.

I reached out and flipped open the dash as I drove. I
stashed the automatic in there. I hooked the revolver out
of my pocket and put that in there, too. I was an arsenal.
I couldn't wait to get rid of the things.

I turned on the air conditioner. I sighed as the first hot
blast turned cool.

"I want . . . I want to kill them," said Georgia with a throaty growl. "I wish I could kill them."

Now there was traffic around me. We were approaching St. Mark's Place. There were people on the street. There were kids with long hair and dyed hair and no hair at all loping up and down the sidewalk to their own rhythm and bop. A light turned red ahead of me. I slowed to a stop. slid out of my jacket. I pushed it at her.

She took it. Her sobbing had worn down to a sniffle now. She put the jacket on and buttoned it up in front. She clasped it closed at the neck with one hand.

Her teeth were clenched. "I wish you had killed them," she said. She bowed her head, crying angrily. "Why didn't you? Why didn't you kill them?"

"I didn't want to get them mad," I said.

The light changed. We rolled on, up out of the Village. Up past the downtown parks, the weird buildings that surrounded them. Skyscrapers with crowns and golden pinnacles, vaunting arches, white Greek columns lit by cold blue light: they hung over us at every window.

I relaxed a little. I fed a cigarette into my battered mouth. I offered one to her. She shook her head. I smoked. The smoke tasted good.

And then it all came out of her. "I want to get them, want to get them," she said between her teeth. "I want to get them any way, any way we can. I want you to print that story like you said. I want everyone to know what they did. I want them to go to jail. I want them to die there. I want them to rot and die."

I glanced over at her. She was staring at me wildly, fiercely. The venom in her eyes startled me. She'd earned it, but it startled me all the same when I thought about the corn-fed country girl I'd seen only a few hours before.

"I want them to rot and die," she said again. She seemed to roll the idea around on her tongue. "I want them all to rot and die."

I nodded. I drove. I smoked. We came into Gramercy
Park. "You want me to nail them in the *Star*," I said.

"Yes. Oh, yes."

"They might weather it. It's only ink."

"Oh no, oh no." She shook her head sharply. "Not in
his town. In this town, ink is everything. Everything. You
ould destroy them. I know it. I know you could."

I was cruising past the row of brownstones where her
uilding was. I saw an opening between two parked cars.
 let the Dodge glide into it.

I threw the gearshift into park and shifted to look at
Georgia. I was leaning on the wheel.

"Yeah," I said. "Yeah, maybe I can." Her eyes gleamed
with hope and hatred as she looked at me. I said: "But I
ave to know about the pictures."

The gleam in her eyes went out like a snuffed candle.
he blinked. She turned her face away from me. The light
f a street lamp poured down on her through the wind-
hield. I studied the glow of it on her hair.

"You've got to tell me the truth, Georgia," I said. "You've
got to tell me so I can put it in the paper. So I can show
why Dellacroce would want to have you slapped around
onight. You've got to tell me and when you're through
elling me, you've got to tell the cops. Then maybe—
naybe—we can really nail them for good and all."

When she raised her face to me, the hatred was gone.
There was only fear in her eyes. The fear and violated
nnocence of a country girl in a bad part of the big city.
She tried to speak. She couldn't. Her face began to crumple.
She threw herself into my arms.

"Hey," I said.

She cried against my chest. I felt the tears making my
hirt wet. I looked down at her hair while she cried. I felt
ike an idiot.

I had to reach around her to get my cigarette to the
ashtray. I tossed it in there and let it smoke. That freed my

hands so I could pat Georgia on the back. I patted her o
the back.

"Hey," I said, more softly. I stroked her hair.

"All I wanted was to be an actress," she said.

"I know," I said. I even sounded like an idiot.

"That's not so awful, darn it. It's not."

"No, it's not awful."

She sniffled. She wiped her nose on my shirt. I'd kin
of liked this shirt, too.

She raised her head. Her eyes were close to mine. The
were nice eyes, soft and deep. Even now, they were nice
filled with tears. I studied her eyes and her bruises and he
lips, puffy with crying. She looked hurt and sad like a littl
girl.

"I was so scared tonight," she whispered.

"I know," I said. "But it's okay. It'll be okay."

"So scared."

"I understand."

"I do want to tell you the truth."

"All right."

"I want to, I just . . ."

"You've got to, Georgia."

"The police will think I murdered that man, that Ken
drick man. They'll think . . ."

"Don't worry. I know the cop on the case. He's a goo
one. He'll watch out for you. If he doesn't, I will."

She gazed up at me. I figured she was about nineteen
She was even younger than Lansing.

"Come on," I said. "I'll take you inside. We can tal
there."

She leaned on my chest again. "Oh God, not tonight.
can't take anymore tonight."

I considered it. I kept my arm around her while I con
sidered it. I looked down at her hair. It was past my deadlin
anyway.

"Okay," I said. "I'll just take you inside."

So I took her inside. I took her up the stairs with m

rm around her shoulder. I opened the door while she
eaned against the jamb. I went into the apartment first and
checked it out. There was no one lurking around.

I went to the door. She followed me. She looked small
and childish with my jacket billowing around her. She threw
her arms around me.

"I don't even know you," she said. "I don't even know
who you really are."

I patted her hair. I gently peeled her off of me. "I'll call
you tomorrow," I told her. "We'll have to talk before my
deadline."

She gazed at me some more. "You know," she said, "you
really do have my father's eyes."

Now I felt like an idiot and an old man at the same time.

I listened to her lock the door, then headed back to my
car.

17

It was past midnight. I was beat.

I went back to the office. I battered out some notes on what had happened tonight. I didn't have the energy to write the full story, but I got it down close enough. When I was done, I typed out some instructions on what to do with the notes in the event of my untimely transformation into ground beef. I pointed out that the two guns I'd taken were locked in the bottom drawer of my desk. Finally, I put the envelope on top of the keyboard to McKay's computer terminal.

I waved to the few night folks wandering around the maze of cubicles. I went home.

When I got there, I turned on the air conditioner. Poured myself a drink. Switched on the tube in the bedroom and lit myself a cigarette. I stationed an ashtray on the bedside table just so.

Then I lay down with my scotch glass balanced on my belly. I sipped my drink and smoked my cigarette and watched TV. I thought fondly of the days when they used to play movies on the tube at night. There was nothing on now but cop shows and talk shows. I chose a talk show.

Some starlet was talking about her latest movie. She was very pretty. Lots of yellow hair, perfect features. I wondered if she felt as soft as she looked. I wondered what it would be like to hold her pressed against me. To have her cry, helpless, on my shoulder. To have her say thank you with big, wide eyes.

But then she probably never did those things. So I wondered if she gave good back rubs, instead. I hurt all over.

After a while, my attention drifted. I tried to remember when the day had begun. I recalled my boss telling me I was going to be fired. But that was not the beginning of it. I had opened my front door to Wally Shakespeare and a sock in the nose. But it went back even farther than that. There was that first moment when my radio alarm went off with the news that I had been scooped on my own story. It really had been a long day. A long day and a lousy one.

My eyes began to close now. I jacked them open, thinking of the cigarette. I snuffed it out. Got undressed. I killed the TV and the light. I climbed into bed.

As I let my eyes close again, I remembered that I was going to talk to Georgia tomorrow. That made me feel a little better. I wondered, vaguely, why it made me feel better. Because, I answered, she would give me my story, the scoop I needed to keep my job, to rescue my reputation. That's why I'd gone looking for her in the first place, wasn't it? Wasn't that why I'd taken advantage of her rage and fear to convince her to talk to me?

God, God, I thought, *I hate this story.* It was low and it was dirty and it was making me low and dirty, too. I took a deep breath, let it out, tried to relax. You do what you have to do, that's the thing of it. No one's perfect, no one's clean all the time. You do your work as honestly as you can, and you do what you have to do. I'd turned this story down when it was just a sex scandal, but it was a murder now. It was a story now, and Georgia was part of it. It was my job to get that story, to get it first. It's an honest job. I get paid honest money to do it. I do it well. I do what I have to do.

I was too tired to go on thinking like that. Bullshit takes too much out of me. The chain of my thought began to break apart, the links drifting off in all different directions. Vaguely, I thought of Mayforth Kendrick lying sprawled on his floor with that bullet in him. *No one has the right,* I

thought. I thought of the thug with the harelip. I thought
of his gun in my back and that stairwell door getting closer
and closer. My arm drifted down over the edge of the bed.
That stairwell door. Closer. Closer . . .

As the last of my consciousness faded away, my arm hung
loose, the hand dangled.

And I felt somebody breathing on it.

My eyes opened quickly, wide. I kept my hand where it
was. There was no question about it. There was a puff of
warm air, then another and another. It came in a steady
rhythm that matched the rhythm of my own breath.

Someone was under the bed.

I pulled my hand back up. I rolled onto my side with a
lot of thrashing and moaning, as if I were going to sleep. I
let my breathing steady. I added a slight gurgle to it to
make it sound like snoring. I lay still, snoring, with my eyes
open, watching the side of the bed.

After about a minute, he made his move. He shifted,
grunting. He slithered into the open. I saw the shadow of
his head emerge. I saw it come up over the edge of the
bed. I waited to get a look at the rest of him.

He stood up. He stood up and up. When he was finished
standing, it seemed his head had vanished among the shadows of the ceiling. I thought at first it was Frankenstein,
come to avenge the bullet in the thigh. It was not a pleasant
thought. In fact, it made my stomach turn to jelly. I lay
there, waiting for him to lean down and crush my head
with his bare hands.

He didn't. The giant began moving away. He moved past
the window. The light from the street outside came through
the pane. For a moment, I saw the titan's face bathed in
its garish glow.

I reached out. I turned on the light on my bedside table.

He spun halfway toward me, then froze in the sudden
brightness. He looked down at me from his incredible height
as I struggled to sit up.

"What the hell?" I said.

Wally Shakespeare just stood there stupidly. His jaw loosened. His hand moved a little at his side. I guess this was supposed to be some primitive form of communication.

I tried a primitive form of my own. "You asshole," I said. "What the fuck are you doing in my bedroom?"

"Uh," the big idiot said.

"Christ! Do you know how fucking tired I am? How am I supposed to sleep with you under my bed?"

"Uh . . . gee," he said.

"Why don't you come back in the morning so I can have you arrested like a civilized person?" I reached for my cigarette pack. I shot a new butt into my mouth. I lit it angrily, puffing great clouds of smoke everywhere. "Christ!" I said.

Wally still stood there, still stupidly. His face, with its big round cheeks, was so empty of expression it almost seemed out of focus. It just sort of floated up there around the ceiling above his gargantuan shoulders, never really taking shape. His broad chest heaved as he breathed in fear.

Then, slowly, while I continued to curse him, he began to get angry. I could almost see it well up from his belly and rise into his shock-dulled brain.

He lifted an arm. It was the size of a log. He pointed a finger at me. It was the size of a little log.

"You . . ." he said.

I stopped cursing at him. If anyone else hit me today, I'd wind up in a Home for the Terminally Punched. I sighed smoke and waited for Wally to gather his thoughts.

"You . . . !" he said again. "You've found Georgia, haven't you?"

I gestured with the cigarette. "Yeah. That's right. That's why I wanted the picture of her."

"But you—you tricked me. You're doing a story on her. You're going to put it in the newspaper that she sinned with that man, that she was in pictures with that politician, sinning." He stepped forward. His hand curled into a fist. "Aren't you?" he said.

I drew my knees up under the covers. I rested my arms on them. I smoked. I eyed the creature. "Yeah," I said. "Yeah, probably. Probably that's exactly what I'm going to do."

He took another step forward. His legs touched the foot of the bed. "You said . . . you said you'd call me if you found out anything, if you could tell me where she was. . . . You made that promise right here in the sight of God."

"Okay, son, okay. Look: sit down."

"You tell me where she is. Her soul is in danger of eternal damnation every second she's in this city."

"Yeah, well, that's true enough. True of all of us. But you still better sit down."

Now both his hands were clenched. "Why?"

"Because I'm not going to tell you where she is, and if you're standing up you might be tempted to hit me again."

For some reason, this made sense to him. He thought it over a second, nodded, and backed away from the bed. There was an easy chair in the corner. He propped himself on the edge of its seat. He clasped his hands in front of him, rubbing them together. He glared at me. He waited.

My situation, it seemed to me, hadn't changed very much since this morning. Here I was entertaining the Amazing Giant Fundamentalist again. It was John Wells' prescription for an exciting time: begin and end each day in fear of your life.

"She doesn't want to see you," I said.

This annoyed him. "Oh . . ." he began.

"It's true, man. She's hiding out from you. Specifically from you."

"Oh, Mr. Wells, that's just the devil. Don't you know that? I mean, it's obvious."

"What?"

"The devil. Satan. That's him telling her what to do. That's not the real Georgia. Why, my daddy could have that demon purged from her soul with a single laying-on of hands."

"That's just it, Oral. She doesn't want the demon purged from her soul."

His face went blank again. "Huh?"

"She wants to be an actress, man. Now, maybe where you're from that's considered the work of the devil, but around here it's a noble enough calling. It even pays well if you hit it big."

He shook his head. He couldn't believe I was this dense. He tried patiently to explain it to me one more time. "Mr. Wells, Georgia is my fiancée. She's going to come back to Ohio with me. She's going to have my children. She's going to stand by me in the trials of my preaching. I mean, that's a woman's role as prescribed by God."

"Is that what it is?"

"Yes," he said with a vigorous nod. "That's right."

"So that's it. I was wondering what it was."

He laughed. He felt I was beginning to catch on. "So, you see, Satan has put these thoughts into her head to tempt her away from the work of the Lord."

I reached out and snuffed the cigarette in the ashtray by the bed. "Well, it's all clear to me now."

"Finally!"

"You're a fucking lunatic."

"Huh?"

"Listen, Falwell, let me ask you a question: How, as you went about your godly duties, did you happen to wind up hiding under my bed?"

Well, he was a little embarrassed about that. A little bit of red rose to his cheeks. He lowered his eyes. "I didn't come here to hide under a bed," he said. "I came here to talk to you directly."

"Yeah, I remember the last time you did that. I'm really sorry I wasn't home to receive you."

"When I saw you weren't home, I decided there was no time to waste, with Georgia threatened by perdition every moment and all. So I . . . I broke in to see if there was any . . . anything lying around that might tell me if you'd found her, and where she was, only . . ."

"Only I came home."

He hung his head. "Yeah."

"And just how did you find out I'd gotten to Georgia in the first place?"

"My new friends told me."

"The folks on Theater Row."

"That's right."

"Who specifically?"

His head came up. His expression had hardened. "Look, that's not the point here. . . ."

"Yeah," I said. "Yeah, it is. I mean, you're sitting here and you're talking like the fruitcake you are about Georgia and Satan and how she's sinning and all that. But you're the one who broke in here, Swaggart. You're the guy trying to look at things that aren't yours, hiding under beds. . . ."

He shot up out of the chair. He towered over my bed. He pointed that big finger at me again. "You listen here, you listen to me!" he thundered. "I may be crazy and I may be a sinner and maybe I can't say things the way you-all can all sharp and smart and—and deceitful, and maybe I sound funny to you talking about God and all . . ." He caught his breath. "But at least . . . at least . . . I *care* about her. I *love* her. I mean, you, with all your talk, all your twisting and perverting things, why, you're just trying to deceive me so I'll leave her to you—"

"Wally."

"You're trying to deceive her so you can write your filthy stories. You're trying—"

"Walter."

"—to use her, to bury her under your lust for sex and scandal in this fiend-haunted city. You're trying—"

"Wal."

He stammered, fell silent. He had run out of words. He was only a student preacher after all. He stood above me with his finger still jabbed at my face. His shoulders rose and fell with his breath.

"Wally," I said quietly. "She doesn't want you, man. She just doesn't want you."

He stood another moment. The fury faded from his eyes. The insecurity came out behind it. A young man's fear. Maybe every young man's fear.

"I'm sorry, pal," I said. "But she's got to go her own way. People have got to go their own ways."

His hand lowered slowly to his side. "But a woman . . ." he said weakly.

"Women, too," I said. "Gotta go their ways. It's not Satan. It's not even me. It's just . . . what it is. It is what it is."

His mouth hung slightly open. He looked like I'd hit him. He took a slow step back, then another. He sank down onto the chair again. He brought his hands up and pressed the heels of them against his forehead. He looked pretty bad, and I felt bad for him. I'd sat in just that posture over more than one woman in my time.

"Sorry," I said. I reached out for another cigarette. I leaned back against the wall as I lit it. He just kept sitting there like that. The poor bastard. "Look, uh, there's other women, you know. Plenty of girls feel just the way you do about things and you find one and you go your way together. You know?" It was the best I could do. One divorce and a few dozen disasters did not qualify me to be a counselor on young love.

Wally threw his hands down on his lap. "You don't understand," he said. "Georgia and me, we . . . we did things. . . ."

"I do understand."

"We . . . we . . . got engaged. . . ."

"That just ain't engaged, Wally. Hell, even engaged isn't engaged. People change their minds all the time. It's just words, man."

"It's *holy* matrimony," he whined.

"Yeah, okay. But it's just words unless they want to be there. Believe me: I know about this part."

This seemed to reach him a little. He looked me over with some interest as he sat there forlorn. "You mean, you were married?"

"I was married," I said. "I was very young and I met a very beautiful, very rich young lady and she wanted to show her daddy that she didn't care which of her suitors he liked. And she was very beautiful and I was very young and that was fine. I knew that's why she was doing it. I went along anyway. Hell, I'd have done a lot more than that for her. She was very beautiful. And I was very young." I dragged in some smoke. "But I guess it wasn't much of a reason for a wedding, was it?" I asked him. And when he shook his head, I said: "Neither is yours."

"But . . ." said the soon-to-be-reverend Wally.

"If you sinned, go wash yourself in holy water," I told him. "Take a pilgrimage. Take an aspirin. Take a long vacation. But don't hold her to an old promise, man, because it won't make things all right when they go all wrong, finally. And by that time, there might be a gir . . . a kid around to go down with you."

He kept looking at me. "I gotta find her," he said. But he didn't sound so sure now. I couldn't tell what he was thinking. I couldn't tell if he was thinking.

"Go home to Ohio, pal. That's Mother Wells' advice. And you can start by getting the fuck out of my apartment."

He just kept looking at me. "I gotta think on this," he said slowly. "I gotta think on this."

"You do that," I said. "But somewhere else."

He stood up. Up and up. He nodded his big head on his big shoulders. His big body started moving toward the door.

I watched him go. I waited. I heard the door slam. I reached out and turned off the bedside light again. I lay down and pulled the covers up under my chin. The air-conditioning was kicking in now and it was downright cool in here.

I closed my eyes. I heard Wally's voice again. He was gone now, but in my head I still heard his voice.

You're trying to deceive me so I'll leave her to you. You're trying to deceive her so you can write your filthy stories.

"Oh shut up," I murmured.

And the long day was over.

18

I stumbled into the city room the next morning at the crack
of eleven.

"What happened to you?" said Rafferty.

"I fell down a flight of stairs."

"You look it."

"Thanks. Fran!" I shouted.

I went to my cubicle. Fran brought me coffee and the
paper.

"What happened to you?" she said.

"I tripped over a sleeping dog."

"Ooh," she said. "Your face."

"Just give me the coffee."

I drank the coffee. It burned my swollen lips. I lit a
cigarette. My jaw ached when I toked it. I read the paper.
We'd led with the heat. NO RELIEF IN SIGHT, we declared.
We skylined Abingdon's press conference. The *Times* had
led with that, but they didn't have anything new either.
Neither did the *News*. I was safe for another day.

I tossed the paper on the floor. I began digging through
the debris on my desk. I dug till I found the phone. I
dragged the phone to me. The effort made my arm ache.
I picked the receiver up and dialed. I listened to the ringing.
It rang five times. I was about to hang up.

"Hello." It was hesitant.

"It's me, Georgia. It's Wells."

"Oh hi. Hi." Her voice brightened and warmed.

"How are you feeling?"

"Shaky. Shaky, but better. Better, only I cry a lot."

"Good. It's good for you."

"It makes my face puffy."

"I like puffy faces."

She managed to laugh a little. "No, you don't."

"Well, I'll like puffy if you can go for purple."

"Are you purple?"

"Only around the head, torso and legs."

"Oh, I'm so sorry." She sounded sorry. It sounded nice.
Does it hurt a lot?"

"Yes."

"Oh, poor guy."

"More, more. Sympathize."

She laughed. "I do. I sympathize."

I smiled at the phone. "Let's talk," I said.

There was a pause. "Okay."

"Don't be too enthusiastic. It'll go to my head."

"I'm sorry. It's just . . ." She lapsed into silence.

"Let me come by."

The silence lengthened. Finally, she said: "Tonight."

I had to fight back a curse. "Tonight's too late," I said.
My deadline's eight o'clock."

"Oh, but can't it wait a day? Just another day."

"No."

"But why?" she pleaded.

Because if I got scooped on this one, I'd be through. But
didn't tell her that. I said: "Georgia, it's news. And it's
good insurance against acts of God and Marino."

More silence. "I just . . . I need time, Mr. Wells." Her
voice had begun to tremble. "I need time."

I listened to her breathing. *I could run it without her,* I
thought. I had the name, I could identify her myself. But
did not want to do that. I was sure she was a victim in
his thing, and I did not want to put her name in the papers
without telling her side of the story.

I wrestled with the angel for a minute. If I were a younger man, I'd have taken him easy. Either the angels were getting tougher or I was slowing down.

"When?" I said finally.

"What about seven?" she said. "That's enough time. I promise I'll tell you everything. I really will. I promise. I just . . . I just have to . . . get myself together." She barely got out a last: "Okay?"

I closed my eyes, nodded. Seven. I could still make the bulldog if I phoned it in. It would be tight, but I could do it. Besides—maybe I could get a hot angle somewhere else. Maybe I could get a job somewhere else. So what if Bush blackballed me? I hear the *Ellenville Register* is always shorthanded.

"Okay, kid," I said.

I heard the start of tears. "You're a nice man, Mr. Wells."

"Call me John when you lie to me," I told her.

I hung up. I sat back. I killed one cigarette. I lit another.

"What happened to you?"

I looked over my shoulder. It hurt my neck. McKay was there, leaning against the edge of the doorway.

"I hammered in a nail with my face," I said. "Didn't you read the notes I left you?"

"I just got in. I had an interview with a former mental patient who rode from San Francisco to New York on a unicycle."

"Sounds like a future mental patient."

McKay laughed. "He was raising money for a charity."

"I'm deeply moved. Go read the notes."

"Hey, you ever try to sit on one of those things? God, your face looks awful."

"At least I have an excuse."

"I think I'll go read the notes."

"Bye."

I dialed the phone again. Now, it rang ten times.

"Manhattan South. Sergeant Hatch."

"Hey, Sarge, it's Wells at the *Star*. Is Gottlieb around?"

"Yeah, hold on."

I held on. Gottlieb picked up. "Don't be happy," he said.

"Believe me, Fred. I'm not happy."

"Good."

"Why aren't I happy?"

"Who could be happy when he looks like a fool and a liar?"

"Not me."

"So don't be happy."

"I'm telling you: it's not a problem."

"Right."

"I take it you haven't found the Abingdon pictures," I said.

"No naked Abingdon pictures. No naked lady pictures. No naked Abingdon with a naked lady. Right now, as far as the New York City police department is concerned, you're a person who has sex fantasies about Senate candidates."

"Terrific."

"And, just so you shouldn't even think of happiness, there's more."

"Oh good. For a minute there, I flirted with the thought of contentment."

"Don't flirt. It looks like Kendrick was starting a modest business in the neighborhood of Avenue A."

"Prostitution."

"A terrible thing."

"So you think he stepped on Alphonse Marino's toes and Alphonse Marino stepped on his throat."

"This by Alphonse is *quid pro quo*, yes," Gottlieb said.

I pinched the bridge of my nose. A mob rubout of a small-time pimp. No pictures. No other leads. I was going to look pretty bad in tomorrow's editions. "You gonna make a statement today?" I asked him.

"Statement! It's already leaking all over the place. What can I do? It's a terrible situation. Who knows what'll happen?"

"Those pictures exist, Fred, I'm telling you. And Marino is looking for them."

There was a pause. "You know this?"

"It's as plain as the welt on my face."

"Ah," he said carefully. "This welt. Is this something maybe your friendly neighborhood detective should be informed about?"

I sighed heavily. "Yeah," I said. "But not yet."

"Eesh," said Gottlieb.

"Yeah," I said again. I hung up. I laid my head back in the chair, my eyes closed.

"Jesus. What happened to you?"

"I danced with a guy named Moose," I said angrily.

I swiveled around in my chair. It was Cambridge. He was wearing an off-gray pinstripe suit. It was perfectly pressed. The striped tie on the white shirt was perfectly knotted. I wondered how he got from home to work in this heat without getting sweaty and rumpled like me. Maybe he slept here. Maybe he changed clothes once he got here. Maybe he just didn't sweat. Maybe he was secretly dead.

He was carrying a leather folder in one hand, tapping it against the other. This was not a good sign. He was also smiling pleasantly. This was even worse.

"Well," he said sweetly. "I hope you got those bruises pursuing the Abingdon story."

"Something like that," I said. "It was pursuing me."

"Heh heh." He was laughing, I guess. "Heh heh. That's good. Come up with anything?"

"Yeah. But it could take me another day to get it nailed down."

He pursed his lips, shook his head. He looked concerned for my welfare. "Johnny, Johnny," he said. "This is the newspaper business, remember? Tomorrow doesn't mean anything."

"Oh now," I said. "It's only a day away."

"Heh heh," he answered. "Well, we've only got until

unday, remember. Although maybe if we show Mr. Bush
hose bruises, he'll give us an extension for good behavior.
What do you think?"

We. Us. My stomach hurt. I grinned at him in answer.
Smoke seeped out between my teeth. Cambridge wagged
a finger at me.

"You know, I'm really going to have to send out a memo
about smoking in here. There's not enough ventilation, and
it's really bad for everyone." His eyes were gleaming. Like
polished steel. He'd never had this much fun before in
his life. "You know," he said quietly, gently, "when this
blows over, things are going to be a lot different around
here." He nodded thoughtfully. He tapped the leather folder
against his hand. I grinned and grinned. I kept grinning as
he walked away, nodding and tapping, into the cubicle
maze.

I stopped grinning. "Eat shit and die," I muttered. I
swiveled around. I picked up the phone. I dialed.

The phone rang once. Then a young woman's voice chirped:
"Abingdon Campaign Headquarters."

It was a long shot, but until Georgia came through, it
was all I had. "This is John Wells at the *Star*." I waited for
her to hang up. She didn't. "I want to talk to him," I said.

"Hold on one moment please." The woman was not chirp-
ing anymore. She was speaking one icy syllable at a time.

I waited. I put out my cigarette. I waited some more. I
pulled out a new cigarette. I toyed with it. I waited. There
was a click.

"Hello?" I said. I expected a dial tone. I got a voice
instead.

"This is Paul Abingdon."

I lit the cigarette. I didn't want the sound of surprise in
my voice. "How're you doing, Congressman?"

He answered quietly, precisely. "Not as well as I was a
few days ago."

"No. No, I guess not."

"What do you want, John?"

"I want an interview." I waited for the slam of the re
ceiver.

"Two-thirty," said Abingdon at once. "Here."

"Well, I . . ." He hung up. I stared at the receiver. Wha
the hell, I asked myself, was that all about? The receive
started humming at me. I set it down in the cradle. I stare
at it some more. I swiveled to one side and stared at it ou
of the corner of my eye. A new voice came from outsid
my cubicle.

"What happened to you?"

"I got beat up," I said. "All right?"

"It's all right with me," said Lansing.

I turned to her. She flinched when she saw the damag
straight on. Then she cursed and shook her head and he
long hair fantailed. She stamped her foot. She put her fis
to her waist. "Did you go to a doctor, John?"

"What doctor? What are you talking about?"

"Did you put anything on . . . ? Oh Christ, Wells, di
you even wash it?"

I reached up and touched the painful places on my face
"I don't know. I mean, I showered this morning. What am
I supposed to do?"

Lansing stepped up to me. She touched my forehead
Her fingers were cool and gentle. The smell of her wa
sweet and when she leaned down to me I could breathe al
of it. I could look way down into her eyes.

"Ouch," I said.

"You need stitches on that, Wells. I'm serious."

"Stitches. I didn't need stitches before you started goug
ing me. Jesus, Lansing."

She stamped her foot again. "It's not funny."

"All right, all right. It's not funny."

"What happened?"

"Alphonse Marino happened. That guy is off my Christ
mas list for sure. I mean it."

"That's going to get infected," said Lansing, looking a

he gash on my cheek. "What's he doing knocking around
reporter? Dellacroce hates that."

"Well, then Dellacroce and I have a lot in common. Not
o mention we both want to get our hands on those pho-
ographs of Abingdon. Last night I found the girl who was
n them. Unfortunately, Marino intercepted her. Kendrick
aust have blabbed about her. Anyway, I had to get her
ut. The girl I mean. I had to shoot a guy."

Lansing let out an exasperated sigh. She released my
ruises and sat down on the edge of my desk. She crossed
er arms. "You shot a guy?"

"Yeah, a big guy too. Looked like Frankenstein."

"You kill him?"

"Hell, no. Are you crazy? I was lucky I hit him."

She lowered her head to her chest. "Dellacroce's gonna
e thrilled."

"I know. But he won't do anything about it once we run
he story. If he does, Maldonado's through, which is just
vhat he doesn't want. Anyway, I'm hoping he'll be more
issed at Marino for bungling it than at me. Stop looking
t me like that, Lansing."

"Well, at least you've got your story anyway," she said
ullenly. "That ought to keep you out of Dutch with the
osses for a while."

"Uh . . . yeah," I said.

She eyed me. "What?"

"Nothing. I got it. It's all right," I said.

"Yeah? So?"

"Well, the girl's a little reluctant to talk."

"The girl with the scarf. So what? You saw the pictures.
f you're sure . . ."

"Oh, I'm sure. But it's my word against hers," I said,
vithout much conviction.

"Your word's good," said Lansing. "Especially if you write
bout what happened last night."

"Look, I've got till tomorrow," I told her. "I'll play it by
ar."

She came off the desk again. Her skirt spun out as sh
pivoted to me. "Wells! What are you talking about? Yo
haven't got till anything. Every reporter in town is afte
this story. You've got it. You can't afford to get beat on i
You can't let yourself get scooped on your own story twice.

"Okay. But the girl's had a hard time of it, Lansing. If
can get her to talk to me, get her side of it in there . . .
just don't want her to come off like a bimbo." I put m
hand to my forehead. It was beginning to ache. "I don
know. Maybe I'll get myself killed before I get myself fire
It'll ease the blow of losing my job."

"I can't believe I'm listening to this. Wells, you can't le
tomorrow's paper run without this story."

My head throbbed. Too many people on my case th
morning. My throat hurt, too. I had smoked too much.
jabbed out my latest. "Look, forget it, Lansing, okay? It
not your problem. I'll figure it out. Forget it." I swivele
back to my phone. I plucked the receiver from it. I starte
to dial. I looked over my shoulder. Lansing was still there
The color had risen in her high white cheeks. Her blu
eyes flashed at me.

"You know," she said. "I get really sick of you some
times."

I hung up. Faced her. "Oh yeah? Well, you're not havin
one of your best weeks either, sister, all right?"

She leaned toward me, both fists at her waist now
"You're . . . you're arrogant!" she said.

I gazed at her. "I'm arrogant. Half of me's dead and th
other half's on relief. How am I arrogant?"

"You're arrogant, and you're . . . bullheaded."

"You lose your way to your desk, Lancer? Get out
here."

She straightened at that. Her cheeks got redder still, bu
her eyes stopped flashing. They were swimming now. "Yo
talk about all this like you're being so . . . noble or some
thing," she whispered. "Is that what you're supposed t
be? Noble?"

I waved her off. "Yeah, yeah," I said.

"With your typewriter and your . . . your fistfights and all this bravado with the mob and everything. You get all . . ."

"What bravado? I'm covering . . ."

"You get all the young people in here to worship you. . . ."

"I'm covering a story. Anyway, I can't help that."

". . . and it's all bullshit, isn't it?" A tear spilled down her cheek. She swiped at it angrily with the filmy sleeve of her blouse. "It's all bullshit. You're not noble. You're not noble, you're . . . you're self-destructive, that's what you are."

"Oh, thank you, Dr. Freud. Now buzz off."

"Wells! You have no *right* to jeopardize your job like this. You have no right to let Cambridge make a fool of you. We need you here. . . ."

"No one's . . ."

"We need you here to stop him from turning the paper into a comic book."

"No one's making a fool of me."

"The hell they're not!" she hissed. She would've shouted it, but we were already drawing glances from outside the cubicle. "He is . . . and she is, too."

"Who?"

"This girl . . ."

"What are you talking about: You don't even know her."

"I don't have to know her."

"Oh great."

"I mean, *look* like a bimbo." She was still hissing. "She *is* a bimbo, you idiot."

Now I started hissing back. "What do you know about it?"

"What did she do, cry for you? She throw herself into your arms?"

I got out of my chair. Lansing took a step backward. But then she dug in. I moved in close to her, but she held her ground.

"Listen . . ." she hissed.

"Look," I hissed. We sounded like a couple of steam

heaters. Curious reporters wandered by outside. Peered i
at us. Passed. "I've been taking shit from you all week,"
said.

Lansing's mouth fell open. "Oh! Oh, *you've* been takin
it? You . . ."

"That's right, and I've had it. All right?" I cut the air wit
my hand. "I've had it!"

"I've been listening . . ."

"Friendship only goes so far!" I hissed.

"Oh, I know it does! I know it does! Everything onl
goes so far with you!" she hissed back.

"What the hell does that mean?"

We were nose to nose. The tears were streaming dow
her cheeks. "You never get close to anyone!" she said. "Yo
never go all the way for anyone!"

"Maybe you want too much from me!"

"I don't care! I don't care! You don't have the right!'

"What the . . ."

"I don't care if it's your dead daughter or this . . . *stupi*
half-life you live or . . . It doesn't give you the right to b
above everything, to hold back from everything. Not from
everything, and not from me!" She retreated a step. He
hands came up to cover her face. Her shoulders shook. Sh
cried hard.

I stood there stupidly, silenced mid-hiss. Why was every
body crying at me all of a sudden? What had I done t
them?

I reached out for her. I touched her arm. She shrugge
me off. "Leave me alone."

"What's going on here?" I said. "What the hell is goin
on with you, kid?"

She lowered her hands. She tried to compose herself
She did not succeed. Still, she managed to reclaim som
dignity. She stood erect anyway. She faced me again, thoug
her eyes were swollen and blurred, her cheeks streake
with mascara.

"What is it, Lancer?" I said again. "What are we fighting about here?"

Again, she trembled on the brink of breaking down. "Nothing," she whispered. "Nothing. Just congratulate me, Wells. Okay? Congratulate me."

"What?"

"I'm getting married."

Then she turned and strode swiftly from the city room.

19

She headed down the hall. I went after her. I wove through
the office maze with the eyes of every staffer in the place
going after me. Looks of curiosity, gossipy leers. I ignored
all of them. I came into the hall in time to hear Lansing
shut the conference room door. I went to it. I pushed it in.
I saw her collapsed in the chair at the head of the table.
She was fighting for control of herself, wiping her cheeks
clean with first one palm then the other.

I came in, shut the door behind me. I lit a cigarette and
perched on the table's other edge. I watched her. She sniffled. She pouted angrily at the table top. She looked up at
me fiercely. The fluorescent light turned crystal, reflected
in the tears in her eyes.

"I met him while I was in the islands. On St. Martin's,"
she said. She caught her breath.

"Okay," I said.

"On the beach."

"Okay."

"He's rich. He's in real estate and he's very rich."

"Okay."

"And he's my age. He's thirty, which . . . well, it's close
enough. And he's handsome." She sniffled again, but the
crying was just about over now. Her hand moved over the
top of her head. "He has hair the color of corn."

"The color of corn," I said. "Okay."

Lansing heaved a big sigh. It shuddered as it came out
of her. "And . . . what else? He's very nice. Very nice,"

she murmured. "My mother likes him." She laughed miserably. "She's been calling me all week to find out if I've made up my mind yet. She's driving me crazy." She brought her hand to her eyes for a second. "I mean, really, Wells. She really is."

"Yeah," I said. "Well: your mother."

"Well, you worked hard to make her hate you," she said.

"It was a Christmas party. I was drunk."

"You could have been nice to her a little bit."

I nodded. "Okay," I said.

Her hands dropped heavily onto her lap, a movement of surrender. "That's it. We were together for a week there. On the island. He says he loves me and he wants to marry me."

I nodded.

"I know it's just a week, but that's what he says."

"Okay."

"So?" She looked up at me. "What else do you want to know?"

I shrugged. "Start with why you're crying."

"Oh, I always cry at engagements."

"Okay."

"I don't know," she said. "I'm confused, that's all. I'm sorry if I've been taking it out on you. I'm just confused."

"What about?"

"Well . . . he wants an answer."

"Give him one."

She stared at me. "Any suggestions?" I said nothing. She looked away. "I don't know, Wells. I don't know how I feel. It's got me all crazy. Really. I mean, I'm a newspaperwoman."

"You can be a married newspaperwoman."

"He lives in Colorado."

"They have newspapers in Colorado."

"He says he wants to move to California someday."

"So you'll work for a magazine."

She laughed miserably. "It's not funny."

"Sorry."

"I mean, he wants to have kids. I want to have kids. Having kids is serious. You have to take care of them."

"So hire someone."

She put a thumb to her chest. "I take care of my kids, Wells."

"Okay," I said. After another moment, I stood up. I reached down and touched her hair. Very soft, her hair.

"You know," I said. "I don't think I can help you with this."

Lansing took a deep breath. "Yeah. I do know."

I stood with my hand on her hair. I tried to think of something else to say. I couldn't. I let my hand fall. I walked to the door.

"I'm sorry," said Lansing.

I opened the door, paused.

"That stuff I said about your daughter and everything. I'm sorry."

I lifted a hand to her. I went out, shutting the door behind me. I stood in the hallway, smoking.

"Damn," I whispered.

20

I left the office. I went to a diner near Grand Central Terminal. I had a grilled cheese sandwich. I stared at it where it lay on the plate. I pushed it around the plate with my fingers. Sometimes I took it off the plate and brought it to my lips. Then I set it down on the plate again. I had a cup of coffee, too. Sometimes I brought that to my lips and stared across the steam. The steam twisted off the top of it. On the other side of the steam, on the other side of the counter, there was a long mirror. I stared at my face in it. It had never been a pleasant face. It was lean and craggy and mean. The widow's peak of gray hair high on my forehead gave it a sharp, almost jagged look. The brown eyes were flat and fierce. It was never a pleasant face, and today it was also battered and purple. The high forehead was split, one cheek was slashed. The whole structure of the thing seemed to have caved in a little, and it made the fierce eyes seem to burn brighter, fiercer still.

I did not look like a happy man, this hot, muggy Friday afternoon. I did not look like a man imbued with the joy of existence. Not quite. I looked—just judging from this superficial image in the mirror, mind you—I looked very much like a man who had missed the last train out of a ghost town.

I sipped a little coffee. It tasted fine.

Lansing had not looked happy either when I left her. But that didn't mean much. She was just being emotional, that's all. Underneath all the rough stuff, she was the emotional type, was our Lansing. She had a big decision to make and it had her all distraught, that's all. She would look plenty happy soon enough. When she went down the aisle with this handsome, dashing millionaire her mother liked. How could she miss being happy then? She'd be ecstatic. Sure she would. Beautiful, too. Hell, Lansing in white with maybe a veil, maybe some flowers in her hair: it'd be one for the fashion pages. I could picture it. I could see it as if she were standing right there in front of me. It was going to be great

It would be a loss to the paper, though. The *Star* would miss her. She was a good one, there was no doubt about that. She wasn't an old-time pavement-pounder, a senior citizen sleuth like me. She was more like one of those caring types, those sensitive, perceptive journalists who usually get on my nerves. Only Lansing made up for it with some regulation grit and fire.

About six months ago, just as spring came on, she did a series on domestic violence. Cambridge gave it some lurid title like BATTERED WIVES: WHAT GOES ON BEHIND CLOSED DOORS. Still, it was a good series, solid stuff all the way After it ran, a lawyer called up, and asked Lansing if she'd do a piece on his client, a woman named Barbara Dell. Dell had been charged with attempted murder. She'd stabbed her husband Larry in the chest with a steak knife. This lawyer claimed Dell had only been trying to defend herself against the man, who'd been banging her around for years.

Lansing spoke to Mrs. Dell. The woman swore she'd reported the abuse to the proper city agency again and again. But she was black and she was poor and she'd gotten nowhere. The agency claimed they did not have a record of her reports.

Lansing checked it out. She went after the people in the agency, the workers, the underlings. She went to see them at home. She convinced them she could be trusted, and that she gave a damn about what she was doing. After a while, some of them started to open up. Some of them even went into the files for her.

One night during that time, Lansing drove home from work and parked her little Honda Accord in her apartment garage. She was about to turn off the ignition when she looked up into the rearview mirror—and found herself staring into the angry eyes of Larry Dell. From the back seat of the Accord, Larry Dell explained how displeased he was about the work Lansing was doing. He even showed her a switchblade to impress his displeasure on her. Lansing was impressed. She was so impressed she stepped on the gas pedal and ran the Accord into the wall of the garage. Dell was still pulling his face out of the front seat as Lansing ran up the driveway to the attendant. Dell got away. Lansing stuck to the story.

In about two weeks, Lance had herself a genuine grade A cover-up. As good as any I've seen. Mrs. Dell, it turned out, was telling the truth. She had reported the abuse and the city hadn't done a thing about it. When Mrs. Dell finally took after her husband with that steak knife, a couple of agency supervisors got nervous about losing their jobs. They hit on the bright idea of pleading ignorance to the whole thing. Lansing nailed their hides to the barn door and Barbara Dell was cleared.

But Larry Dell was not arrested. The case was cold, the D.A.'s office said. Whatever proof of abuse had existed was gone now. It was impossible to make a case.

By then, of course, Barbara Dell was not living with Larry anymore. She and her two kids had moved in with her mother in an apartment in Washington Heights. About two weeks after the charges against her were dropped, she was found dead in the bedroom of that apartment. She'd been beaten and stabbed repeatedly. Larry Dell was charged with the murder.

I came into the office one night late and found Lansing sitting alone in her cubicle. She was sobbing. She wasn't just crying. She wasn't dabbing the occasional tear with a handkerchief. She was leaning forward in her swivel chair as if she'd been sucker-punched. She was rocking herself and sobbing and sobbing. Bawling like a child.

I perched on her desk. "We just tell them," I said to her. "We don't make them up, ya know."

She fought for control. It took her a long time. Finally, when she could speak, she looked up at me. I expected her to tell me how guilty she felt. Or how it broke her heart to have her work go for nothing. Or how it made her ache to see a life lost to the stupidity of government drones. She did not tell me any of that. She said only: "They're mine, Wells. Every last one of them. Every last one of them is mine."

It was a bloodbath. The city never stood a chance. Seven people resigned because of the stories she wrote in the next few weeks. One was an agency head, one was an assistant D.A. She'd have nailed two more, I think, if the mayor hadn't gotten his rich friends to lean on Bush who leaned, in turn, on Cambridge. By then, anyway, vengeance had been hers. She was satisfied. I drove her to the cemetery the day she laid flowers on Barbara Dell's grave.

I drank my coffee. I stared at the mirror across the counter. Lansing was good all right. The *Star* would miss her. So would I.

I don't care if it's your dead daughter or this stupid half-life you live. You don't have the right to hold back from everything. Not from everything and not from me.

"Oh hell," I murmured to myself. I set the cup in its saucer. I lit a cigarette. I rolled the filter between my fingers as I drew in the smoke. *Oh hell*, I thought, *what does she want from me?*

There had been women in my life since my wife walked out on me. There had been women in the six years since my daughter walked off into a forest near her summer camp and hanged herself. There had been enough women to make the nights go by, and some who stayed for nights and nights on end. Some of them I thought I needed. But I did not need them, it turned out. They left and I survived. I thought

I loved some of them, too. But it had not been love, it had
never quite been love. And nowadays, love and need—
they seemed like memories of another man's lifetime. I was
not looking for them anymore. I wouldn't even have known
where to look.

Lansing could not understand that. She was not supposed
to understand. She was twenty-six. She thought everyone was hungry like she was hungry. She thought everyone
yearned the way she yearned. She was supposed to feel like
that, like she would die for someone, like someone would
die for her. All that crap. And when the yearning and
hungering and so on died down, she was supposed to
find someone who could be around for her. Someone handsome. Someone rich her mother liked. Someone young,
her own age.

I was forty-six. I smoked three packs of cigarettes a day,
sometimes four. I had since I was seventeen. I drank too
much some days. Some nights, I slept too little. Some of
the meanest men in the five boroughs lay awake in their
beds wondering what I'd look like with a bullet in my chest.
Lansing did not worry about such things when she pinned
me with those eyes of hers. But I did. When her lips parted
and the black of those eyes got wide at me, I could hardly
think about anything else. I thought about how I'd be fifty
when Lansing was thirty. I thought about how, when she
was thirty-five, I'd probably be dead.

I knew, I guess, what I was to her. I'd given her a break
once. I'd let her cut in on a story of mine and it helped get
her a job on the paper. I'd played her rabbi sometimes since
then, given her advice, stood up for her in the constant
management firefights. I knew she needed someone like
that. I knew her old man had been a D.A. out in Chicago,
one of those crime-busting types, and that he'd died when
she was twelve years old. I knew she needed someone
sometimes to help her figure the angles, and to give her
the high sign when she came through.

But she'd confused one kind of need with another. I knew

that too. And I knew it would be no good in the end if confused her any more.

So I sat at the counter in my diner near the terminal. drank my coffee. I smoked my cigarette. I stared into th fierce and fading face in the mirror across from me. Th sadness, the old sadness and the new, was chiseled into i now. I did not think that that would ever change.

I shook my head at my own reflection.

"Jesus," I said, "what the hell happened to you?"

I paid my tab and headed out. It was time to meet wit Abingdon.

21

The congressman's campaign headquarters were within walking distance. That was too bad: It wasn't a good day for walking. The heat seemed to have thickened overnight. The air itself seemed gray, the color of the rain that would not come. I moved down Lexington Avenue through a flow of sweating faces, of damp foreheads and mouths opened to pull in what breath there was. By the time I reached Thirty-ninth, my jacket was off again, my tie was loosened again, my shirt and shoulders sagged. I was glad to reach the place in the middle of the block.

It was a long storefront. Bunting hung from the sill. Banners in the window. Stars and stripes on the banners. ABINGDON FOR SENATE HEADQUARTERS one banner said. I passed through the glass door and came gratefully into the air-conditioning.

There was a second of murmuring after I walked in: the usual office noise. Then it stopped. From every desk in the room, gazes turned toward me. I stopped at the first desk. A woman in a soft pink dress sat behind it. She was young and bright-eyed, but her glossy lips were set in a frown just for me.

I stood before her, slipping my jacket back on. "Tell him I'm here," I said.

She tilted her head just slightly. "He said to send you back."

Back I went. Down the corridor formed by the gunmetal desks—and the gunmetal stares—on either side of me. An aluminum box had been erected against the rear wall. I rapped on the door of the box, waited for a call, and pushed inside.

The candidate was seated at his desk. Not a gunmetal desk but a wooden one. Better for the photogs, more quaint. His wife was there, standing beside him, bent forward, leaning on the desk over the sheets of paper fanned out in front of them. They were both framed against the maps pinned up behind them. They both had their eyes raised to me.

"Have a seat, John," Abingdon said. He gestured at the green chair in front of the desk. He did not crack a smile.

I sat down. He sat back and pinned me with his piercing blue eyes.

"Still hot out there?" he asked.

"Yeah," I said. "In here?"

He inclined his square, jutting chin slightly. "Hot enough." He came forward, clasped his hands on the desktop. "So. What can I do for you?"

I glanced up at Mrs. Abingdon, her sharp angles hovering above me.

"Anything you have to say to my husband, you can also say to me," she said. The clipped New England tones pattered at me like hail.

I raised my eyebrows at Abingdon. His expression did not change. "All right," I said. "Then here it is. I saw those pictures, Abingdon. You can keep saying they don't exist for a while, but I saw them, I know they do. I guess I thought I'd come by here and give you a chance to make the disclosure yourself. It's a stinking story, and it's all going to come out eventually. If you want to salvage something from it, you're going to have to beat me to the punch."

Abingdon let that lie there a while. Then, very slowly, he said: "In other words, you want me to do your job for you." He opened his hand to me. I kept my mouth shut. "The word is that you're in quite a lot of trouble over this story. It would just suit you, wouldn't it, if I broke down and told all exclusively for the *Star*."

I almost laughed. The congressman was a pro all right. "Well," I said. "It wouldn't hurt."

"No doubt," said Abingdon. "But why should I play along?"

"Well, you haven't exactly made a friend of me so far," I said. "You've called me a fool in public and practically a liar, too. Even if my bosses weren't on my tail, I'd have no reason to hold back on this one. I'm going to find those pictures eventually. You must know that or you wouldn't have agreed to this interview."

The congressman brought his hands up from the desk, the palms pressed together as if in prayer. He rested his chin on the fingertips. "Off the record," he said quietly.

"Yeah?"

"What would it take to make a friend of you again?"

Now I let him wait while I mulled it over. "You wouldn't be trying to buy me off, would you?" I asked him. He didn't answer. "Hell, man, what's the good of that?" I said. "I'm only one wolf in the pack."

"Still," he said, quiet as before. "What would it take?"

He watched me, propped on his fingers. The Mrs., leaning over me, stared until I thought she would burn holes in the side of my head.

"The truth," I said finally. "It would take the truth."

"Ach!" The guttural sound came from Mrs. Abingdon. She pushed away from the desk in exasperation. "The truth! You're a newspaperman. What do you know about the truth?"

I glanced at her. "Mrs. Abingdon, I realize this is hard for you. . . ."

"Oh? Do you?"

It was arctic, but I pushed on. "You've got to understand that it's not personal. I'm just . . ."

"Trying to do your job?"

"Well . . . yeah."

She cocked an eyebrow at me. "And you think I'm being

emotional about a . . . a personal matter between mysel
and my husband."

"It would be understandable," I said.

She charged back at me, leaned over me. "No," she sai
into my face. "No, Mr. Wells, it wouldn't. I have worked
—*worked* with my husband on every campaign he's eve
run, and on every project. There've been no decisions
wasn't privy to, no loss I didn't suffer, no gain I didn't enjoy
Paul and I are more than a mere marriage. We're a team
We work together. No matter what personal issues ther
may be between us."

I cleared my throat. I didn't know what to say.

Mrs. Abingdon warmed to her subject. "Let me tell yo
something," she continued. "Let me tell you somethin
about the truth, my simplistic friend. The truth is that m
husband is going to the Senate. He belongs in the Senate
He's the sort of man they need there. He's strong and he'
a leader and he has a vision of what this country can be an
what it can do. And who's his opponent?" Her bony han
moved through the air on a wave of contempt. "Maldo
nado." She spat the name. "A two-bit criminal with a four
bit criminal behind him. That's the *truth*, Mr. Wells. An
if you succeed in pursuing this story, in destroying m
husband for the sake of some cheap, filthy stories starte
by some dime-store blackmailers, then you will have bee
instrumental in giving the people of New York State a rep
resentative who will be less at home making laws than h
would be making bathtub gin and . . ."

Abingdon made a movement. A slight movement with
one hand. His wife fell silent instantly.

"Mrs. Abingdon has strong opinions on who should b
the senator from New York State," he said.

"That's fine," I said. I looked up into her ferocious gaze
"And I'll be honest with you, ma'am. I don't really give
damn who your husband sleeps with."

"Oh!" she said, furious. "You dirty little . . ."

The congressman gestured her silent again.

"I mean it," I said. "I had a chance for an exclusive on these pictures, remember? I'm the guy who turned them down."

Abingdon still spoke slowly, quietly with the open vowels of Boston. "Then why are you so—so hell-bent on getting your hands on them now?"

"Because way back then it was adultery," I said. "Now it's murder."

"Murder!" Mrs. Abingdon crossed her arms, turned her back on me. She walked across the room to a coffee maker set against the wall. I heard her heels clip-clop on the linoleum. She poured herself some coffee, angrily shook in some powdered creamer.

"Yeah." I stood up. I addressed her back. "It's a slightly different commandment, Mrs. Abingdon."

She whipped around. The steaming white coffee sloshed over the rim of her paper cup. I saw it drip on her hand. She did not flinch. "I didn't know Mayforth Kendrick," she said. "And from what I've read in the papers, I'm quite glad I didn't have the privilege. I find it hard to imagine why the death of a man like that should have anything to do with keeping a man like my husband from having a hand in the affairs of his country."

I looked from her to the man sitting behind the desk. He remained imperturbable as his wife burned and fumed. There was even humor in those blue eyes, and a trace of irony on his lips. It seemed to me just then that he would probably have made a good senator. I faced his wife again.

"Yeah, I can see where you'd find it hard to imagine," I said. I walked to the door. But I turned there. The two of them were staring after me. Mrs. Abingdon's eyes glittered with the force of the stare. "I'm going to get this story," I told them.

The two turned their stares on each other.

"And I'm going to get it soon."

For a breath—then another—the husband and wife searched each other's eyes. Finally, Abingdon looked up a me.

"Thanks for stopping by," he said.

22

n the sidewalk again I lit a cigarette. It tasted sour in the
eat. I tossed it away.

I stuffed my hands in my pockets. I started up the street
ward the terminal. Pushing through the sparse crowds,
gainst the thick heat. Staring at the sidewalk, watching it
immer and steam.

What the hell, I thought. So Abingdon wouldn't talk. I
ill had nothing to worry about. I was all set up, in fact. I
ad the name of the girl in the pictures. I had every news
utlet in town beat on that. And to go with it, I had an
yewitness piece on Maldonado's campaign tactics that would
ave Bush singing in the shower for days. I had nothing to
orry about at all.

Except smearing Georgia Stuart. Once I wrote those sto-
es, she'd be in the thick of it for certain. The little Ohio
irl would find out what it was like to be convicted in the
ress without a chance to testify. To become the punch line
f dirty jokes, and the moral of cautionary tales. She'd see
erself lampooned in satires, and smirked at by comedians
n TV. She'd go to sleep at night and wake up in the morning
earing her name drowned in men's barroom laughter, seeing
er image reflected in women's condemning eyes.

But that was not my problem. I had enough to worry
bout. Bush and Dellacroce, Cambridge and Marino. Mob-
ters and editors: the worst elements of society on my tail.
ust like Lansing said: I couldn't go soft because some bim-
o'd been slapped around a little. Because she'd ruined one

of my better shirts by crying in my arms. If Georgia wante
to tell her side of the story in time for the bulldog editior
she knew how to reach me. I couldn't hold up the grea
march of American journalism just because she needed tim
to collect her thoughts after being kidnapped and torture
and before being stripped naked in every living room i
the country.

I needed a hot angle. I needed to confirm the existenc
of those pictures. And if the cops couldn't find them,
Abingdon wouldn't talk, if Georgia herself couldn't face th
music, where the hell else was I supposed to go?

I stopped. I looked up at the broad facade of the Termina
hanging there in the damp atmosphere. I looked up at th
stone Mercury on its summit as, unconcerned with th
temperature, he spread his arms to the multitude below.
was jostled from behind.

"Move, wouldja," someone muttered.

I took a deep breath, started walking again. I felt like
was working on one of those sliding square puzzles. I use
to do them all the time when I was a kid. You started wit
a picture of Donald Duck or something—a picture draw
over several squares held together in a frame. Then yo
slid the squares around from place to place until the pictur
was all scrambled. Then you tried to put it together again
holding the frame in your two hands and sliding the square
with your thumbs. Even when two pieces clicked togethe
it didn't always help, because you might have to move on
to get another around it. Even as one section of the puzzl
became clearer, another became more of a mess.

Now, as I sweated and huffed my way back to Forty
second Street, two squares clicked together in my head an
I decided to ignore the rest of the picture for a while
Suddenly I had an answer to a question that had bothere
me since the night before. If it led to a new angle fo
tomorrow's editions, that would be enough.

I tried walking faster up the avenue to get to my car, bu
the heat was just too much for me. I pushed it as far as

could go, and was practically gasping as I reached the intersection.

I stopped at a phone booth. I called information to get the address I wanted. I moved around the terminal to Vanderbilt and crawled into the Artful Dodge.

It was a Friday in August: There was almost no traffic at all. The Dart and I rolled easily down into Chelsea. A block of Twenty-first Street, near Ninth. It was a block the gentry hadn't invaded yet, though they had the place surrounded. In the midst of the fancy new eateries and antique stores and preserved brownstones, this was still a stretch where the bricks of the buildings were yellow with grime, where the corner bodega still kept some cockroaches around for the cat to kill. I parked in a tow-away zone, hoping my press plates would keep me safe.

The place I wanted was a flat-faced, four-story rectangle of brick. The iron banister flanking the stoop was rusted orange. One end of it had pulled free of the concrete. When I put my hand on it, it vibrated and swayed to the side. I went up gingerly. I pushed through a glass door into the vestibule. I scanned the list of names above the doorbells. I pressed the button under the name Susan Scott.

She was the waitress from Cole's restaurant on Theater Row. She was the one who'd given me Georgia's address.

Her muffled voice came out of the door speaker in a burst of static. I shouted my name back at her. I had to wait almost half a minute before the inner door unlocked. I pushed inside.

She lived on the third floor. The flights were long. The hall was hot. I reached her door and leaned against the jamb, panting. I knocked. I had to wait a full minute this time before I heard her footstep come near.

Susan Scott pulled the door back and stood aside. I stepped into a room the size of a corridor. The sofa against one wall and the two chairs against the wall opposite were so close together that her guests must have sat knee to knee. There was a bookshelf on the third wall and a kitchenette in the

fourth. There was an entrance to the bedroom squeezed in
between the rest.

Susan shut the door. She turned and leaned back against
her hands as they clutched the knob.

She was wearing a bathrobe. The hem of a nightgown
trailed out from underneath. The getup didn't do much for
her figure, and she wasn't wearing any makeup either. But
she was still stunning with her rich black hair touseled and
wild, and her rich lips pursed in a smile at me.

"Fancy meeting you here," she said. Her whiskey voice
was sharp, sardonic.

I nodded. I was still trying to catch my breath. "I re
membered you worked nights," I said. "I hope I didn't
wake you up."

"No, no, I was just . . ." She made a half gesture toward
the living room. Then she stopped it, let her hand fall. "You
look beat. Can I get you some water or something?"

"Yeah, please."

She walked past me. I caught the light scent of toilet
water trailing behind her. She glanced up at me shrewdly.
I watched her go by.

She stood at the sink with her back to me. She reached
up to a cupboard for a glass. I stopped watching her. I
turned and let my eye pass over the living room again. I
saw a coffee mug set down on the wooden floor next to the
sofa. I shifted a little. I saw another mug by the leg of one
of the chairs.

Susan was running the water now. Waiting for it to cool.
I moved to the bedroom entrance. I snuck a look inside.

The place was in shadow, the lights out, the shades drawn.
But I could make out a frame bed with the sheet rumpled
at the center of it. The room was so small that the bed took
up most of it. There was a thin writing table against one
wall, and a wooden chair pressed in to it tight. I saw the
outline of a closet door that did not look like it could open
without hitting the bed. There was also, beginning in one
corner, a brief hallway with a bathroom at the end of it.

Susan turned from the sink quickly. I looked at her.

"Nice place," I said.

She stepped back to me. Handed me the water. "Small," she said. I drank. "Now, is there something you want . . . or is this how reporters ask for dates?" I came gasping out of the water. "You're a little old for me, you know." She took the glass from me, held it.

"I really came to ask you a question."

"You couldn't phone?"

"It's not the sort of question you ask on the phone."

"Okay. Shoot."

"Is Wally Shakespeare hiding under your bed?"

My hand shot out and caught the glass before it could hit the floor. I gave it back to her.

She had gone pale, but she still managed a wry twist to that rich mouth. She still managed to snort a little before she turned her back on me again and returned, stiffly now, to the kitchen counter.

"He does that, you know, our Wally," I said. "It's a favorite of his and he strikes me as the kind of guy who sticks with something if it works for him."

She did not turn, but I saw her nodding.

"On the other hand," I went on. "I notice your bed isn't very high off the floor and Wally is a big fellow, all right. Still, Susan, even if he's not here, I'd appreciate an answer."

She set the glass down. I heard the thump as it hit the linoleum. She faced me, her back against the counter. There were two spots of color in her cheeks. Her eyes were bright.

"A man has been killed, after all," I said.

"I know that. Don't you think I know that?"

"Yeah. Yeah, I think you do."

"I just . . . I just don't want to be in the newspapers, that's all. It's all so . . . so sordid."

"You could talk to the cops," I said. "I mean, you'll have to eventually."

She winced. "Do you think so?"

"Depends what you've done."

"She hasn't done a thing," said Wally Shakespeare.

I cast my eyes heavenward. There was a loud click from the bedroom. The closet door swung open. It went about halfway then hit the bed. Wally grunted as he squeezed and twisted his enormous form out into the room. No wonder it had taken Susan a while to buzz me in.

When the giant emerged, he shut the door and sidled between bed and wall until he came around to my side of the room. He stepped out into the living room. His heavy arms drooped sheepishly. There was a hangdog expression on his country mug.

I shook my head at him. "Wally, Wally, Wally," I said.

"Dang it. Dang it, Mr. Wells. How the heck did you know I was here?"

"When you showed up under my bed last night, old friend, you said your pals on Theater Row had told you I'd found Georgia. It didn't figure. How could you be hooked in deep enough to know that and not know where she was?" I tilted my head at Susan Scott. "Unless the same person who'd given me her address was going to a lot of trouble to hide it from you."

Wally's jaw dropped. His big dumb country face looked even bigger and dumber than before. For a long moment, he just stood there and gaped at me. Then he turned and gaped at Susan. She averted her eyes. She looked down at the imitation brick of the kitchenette floor.

"I'm sorry," she whispered.

"You knew?" he said, amazed.

I shuffled a cigarette out of my pack and into my mouth. I lit it. I sighed out smoke. I suspected this was not going to be the most pleasant visit I'd ever made.

"You knew?" said Wally Shakespeare again. He took a lumbering step toward her.

Susan nodded at the floor. She closed her eyes.

"You . . . you knew?"

"She knew, Wally. For Christ's sake. Could we move on here?" I said.

He ogled me. He ogled her. "You told me," he said. "You told me to come stay with you. You told me I could come sleep on your couch. You told me not to worry about Georgia, that you'd ask around. Ask your friends. They'd be sure to turn her up eventually, you said. And I stayed here and . . . and last night . . . last night, you . . . you *kissed* me, Susan. I *let* you kiss me. And I'm engaged, oh God, oh God, this city is steeped in sin, oh Father, oh Father . . ."

"Oh brother," I said.

Wally threw his giant hands out at either side. One word hung on the edge of his open mouth before he finally dropped it on us:

"Why?"

Susan stood there with her face turned away, her chin pressed to her shoulder. She stood there with her eyes closed and I saw her eyelashes grow damp though the tears didn't fall.

"Why?" said Wally. He threw his hands out even farther. "Why?"

She would not turn to him. She only waved him off with a hand. "Just . . . never mind," she said.

"But . . . but why?" said Wally.

"Because she likes you, Einstein," I said.

He gawked at me again. I was getting sick of it. Susan lifted her chin, opened her eyes. She shook her head. "Don't tell him that," she said. "Don't tell him that. He's so . . . simple . . . he'll just believe you."

"It's true, isn't it?" I said.

"Well . . . yes . . . I mean . . . Now it is." She hiccupped a little. She said to him: "It's true now, Wally, it really is. I really do like you now, but—" She struggled with it. Wally continued to stand there like a ten-ton jackass. I continued to smoke, grateful for something to do. She went on: "But I don't want to lie to you anymore. Okay? I mean, at first . . . at first, it was just to get back at Georgia."

"Get back at Georgia?" said Wally, with that debonair flair we'd all become so used to.

Susan let out an exasperated, "Oh!" She ran her hands up through her mane of hair. "I hate this. I hate this stupid city. I hate this stupid business. I . . . am so sorry, Wally. I am just . . . so . . . sorry." She sighed. "About four months ago, okay? I met a guy. He was the first nice guy I had met in this town in . . . since I came here from Vermont."

"Paul Abingdon?" I asked.

"No." She sounded annoyed. "I don't make it with married men. This stupid city still hasn't done that to me. This was a guy named Allen Simon. He worked on Paul Abingdon's campaign. That was how I knew Georgia's address, because she got to apartment-sit for him while he moved up to Albany to run things there." I nodded. I remembered the name on Georgia's mailbox. "So this was . . . like . . ." She lifted her hands as she searched for the right words. "I mean, nice. Okay? I mean, to be around these people, they all had nice clothes and nice apartments and nice friends. And it was nice, after hanging around trying to get a part, dealing with other actresses, everyone complaining and angry and jealous of each other, it was just . . . nice, that's all."

I'd never heard politicians described that way before. But then I hadn't been around actors too much either.

Susan went on as Wally stared and stared at her. "So, you know, one day, he came into Cole's to pick me up, and there was Georgia and . . ." She looked up at the ceiling, fighting back the tears. "And she came on to him. I mean, they hit it off. I guess that's what it was. I mean, it sure did seem to me like Georgia came on to him, but she says . . . I mean, she says they just . . . hit it off. And, anyway, pretty soon . . . you know: They were going out together. Allen and Georgia instead of Allen and me."

"Allen and Georgia!" exclaimed Wally. "But—but we're engaged."

"Would somebody deliver the news to this clown? I can't believe this," I muttered. I could not help myself.

It was easier for Susan to go on now. It seemed to be

flowing out of her on a current of relief. "Then, about a month later . . . when you came to town . . . Wally, when you started asking about Georgia, and I found out who you were . . . At first, I was thinking— Oh, I don't know what I was thinking at first. I guess I told myself it would be, like, some kind of a joke, like, you know, turnabout is fair play and everything. I decided . . . you looked so simple . . . so innocent . . . I decided I'd get you to stay here . . . keep you away from her, and maybe . . . maybe take you for myself for a while. Sort of like . . . well, like . . . revenge."

"My God in heaven!" said Wally.

I made a similar remark.

"But then . . . just this last day or so . . . you know . . . I really did get to . . . like you, you know, Wally. I mean, you really are . . . sweet? simple?" She gave a wry shake of the head, almost smiling. "You're a breath of fresh air in this city, I'll tell you that much." The trace of a smile faded from her lips under the remorseless weight of his stare. "But then . . . then . . . that Kendrick man got killed . . . murdered. I didn't know what I was supposed to do. When you told me you thought Georgia was the girl in the pictures, I didn't know if I should go to the police myself, or tell you to go to the police or . . . or what?"

"Which is when I showed up," I said.

She nodded, lowering her eyes. "Wally told me he was going to see you, Mr. Wells. When you showed up asking for her, I figured . . . if I told you how to find her . . . well, you're a reporter . . . you'd find out the truth and then the police would know everything that I could tell them anyway. . . ."

"Then why'd you tell Wally that I'd been around?" I asked.

Susan Scott shuddered. "Because I wanted him to know the truth about Georgia, but I was afraid you'd tell him yourself and then he'd figure out the truth about me and then . . . Oh!" She put her hands to her temples, let them drop again. "I feel like such a stupid, stupid . . . I guess I was just so angry at her, I didn't think. I didn't think."

Slowly, Wally Shakespeare's mouth closed. Slowly, he moved out of the bedroom doorway. He clumped into the living room and dropped down onto the sofa. He sat there with his shoulders hunched and his eyes on the floor.

"I can't get all this into my head," he said. "You mean . . . you mean, you did all this . . . kept me away from Georgia . . . and lied to me and . . . and all that . . . because you *like* me?" He raised his dunderheaded eyes to her. She nodded. He lowered his dunderheaded eyes. He thought. "I guess . . . I guess that's kind of *nice*. Isn't it?" He raised his dunderheaded eyes to her. She smiled a little. He smiled back.

This had all the makings of a tender scene. I hate that. I headed for the door.

I headed out to see Georgia Stuart.

23

Thunder struck when I stepped out into the street again. A long roll of thunder from the distant west. I glanced up hopefully. The sky hadn't changed much. The humidity misted the blazing August sun, but there were no rain clouds. I shook my head, crossed the street to my car where it stood, untowed.

I stripped off my jacket and tossed it inside. I followed it onto the front seat. The old car wheezed at being called into action again so soon. The ancient air conditioner screeched deep in its belts. There was a perilous clanking underneath me as I rolled out of the parking place, around the corner and around the corner again to make our way to the East Side.

Georgia had said seven. It was now only five. I could not hold out any longer. Georgia's name was going to be in my story tomorrow, and Susan's version of events would only make things look worse for her if she didn't explain herself. Ready or not, the Ohio girl had some questions to answer. Had she stolen Susan's guy or simply fallen for him? How had she jumped from him to Abingdon himself? Maybe I'd been wrong. Maybe Georgia wasn't a victim. Maybe she was just a bimbo, like Lansing said. Either way, I wanted her side of the story. And I wanted it for the bulldog edition.

I found a parking spot on Irving Place again. I walked back to Gramercy, to Georgia's brownstone. I came up the stoop and into the vestibule. I pressed the button marked "Simon."

The door unlocked instantly. I pushed inside. It was a swank lobby. Fresh green carpeting with the shape of an urn woven into it. Lanterns hanging from the ceiling. A carved wooden banister running up beside the stairs.

But the heat here was just as oppressive as it had been at Susan's place. The flights were just as long and Georgia was on the fourth floor. My shirt was a mess and my lungs were heaving as I came down the hall to her apartment door.

The door opened before I reached it. Georgia stepped out.

"What do you . . . ?"

She saw it was me and stopped short, fell silent. She pulled the door closed behind her. She did not pull it shut.

I leaned my shoulder against the wall and looked at her. She was wearing a wraparound skirt and a yellow T-shirt. Sweat darkened the shirt, under her arms, between her breasts. Her forehead and her neck were shining with it. Her eyes were shining with fear.

I panted. "You were expecting someone," I said.

"You're early," said Georgia.

I nodded. I saw her lip trembling. Her hand fluttered to her mouth to make it stop. I noticed the bruises on her cheeks: her souvenirs from Marino.

"Don't you have air-conditioning?" I asked her.

"What?"

"You look hot. This is a fancy place. They ought to have air-conditioning."

"I . . . yes, I . . ."

I pushed off the wall. I came forward wearily. Georgia looked up at me as I approached her. Her eyes were still afraid, but they were trusting, too. They searched my face, trusting and innocent like the eyes of a little girl.

"I guess it doesn't matter in this heat," I said. "If you do heavy work in this heat, you sweat, air-conditioning or not."

"I don't . . . understand what . . ."

I reached around her. I pushed the door. It swung in.

I could see beyond her into the apartment. I could see the clothes strewn about in there. I could see the big suitcase open on the floor.

"It's just too damn hot to pack," I said.

Georgia looked down. I walked by her into the apartment.

The air-conditioning was on, and it felt good as it dried the sweat on me. I stood in the middle of the room and looked around. The place was spacious and bright. There were paintings on the walls, abstracts, originals. To my right, there was a chandelier hanging in a dining nook over an oaken table. A sofa and chairs stood at the broad center of the place. They were gathered around a coffee table atop a Chinese rug. That's where most of the clothing was laid out: on the sofa and chairs. The suitcase sat on the rug. All of this was lit by the northern light that came in through a bay window overlooking the street. There was a love seat in the bay.

Georgia came into the room slowly. Her lips were pressed together now, her eyes were still turned down. She closed the door behind her and stood like that, her hands folded meekly on her skirt. She looked like she expected me to scold her.

"You weren't going to be here at seven," I said.

She shook her head.

"Who got to you?"

She looked up, surprised. "Ab . . . Abingdon," she said. "One of his people."

"He gave you money?"

She nodded.

"Cash?"

She shook her head. "A cashier's check."

"Let me see it."

She moved eagerly to a wooden bar against the far wall. There were papers on it. She picked up the top sheet and brought it to me. She stood close to me as I looked it over. I could smell the sweat mingling with her shampoo.

I handed the check back to her. "Not bad," I said. "And you thought he'd come back when I buzzed."

"Yes. But it's not the money—" She stopped.

"What?"

"You won't believe me now, will you? You won't believe anything I say."

"Try me," I said.

She nodded again. She moved past me silently. She walked into the bay and sat down on the love seat. She turned and looked out the window. I saw her profile against the lush green of the trees in the park. She seemed to be looking off somewhere far away.

"Is it—" Her voice wouldn't come. She tried again. "Is it all going to be in the newspaper tomorrow?"

"Yes," I said.

"It's gonna kill my mom and dad." She glanced at me. "I guess I should have thought of that before, huh?" I shrugged. She smiled. "Mr. Wells, you've been so nice to me. You rescued me from those men last night, just like . . . just like some hero on television. I felt so bad when I took that money today, when I said I'd go without talking to you, but . . ." She lifted her shoulder. "I guess I'm a coward. I'm afraid if I talk to you those men will come back looking for the pictures. I don't have them. I really don't."

"I know."

"You know?"

"You'd have told last night if you knew. I would have. Anyone would have."

"Oh." She was quiet a moment, thinking. "Then . . . what is it you want to ask me?"

I lit a cigarette. I leaned against the back of a chair. I looked at her sitting there in the love seat with the park and the August sky behind her. I wondered who she was, who she was really. Lansing said she was a bimbo. Susan Scott said she'd stolen her man out from under her. And yet, standing there, looking at her, listening to her talk, I did not believe it. If she was guilty of anything, it seemed to me, she was guilty of youth and innocence. Of letting people use her. Of letting them scare her. Of letting them tell her what to do.

Once again, I heard the distant roll of thunder. I said: "I just want you to tell me what happened. Your side of the story. That's all."

She stared out the window sadly. She stared in silence a long time. My eyes traced her profile and her figure as she sat. She was very young. Even younger than Lansing. I remembered the softness of her when she'd cried in my arms last night. The softness of her breasts as they'd pressed against me. I thought about Lansing. I felt empty and sad.

Finally, she sighed. "It's not much of a story really, I don't suppose. Not unless you understand where I come from, what I wanted. It's beautiful out west, in Ohio. It really is. Beautiful and green with rolling hills and wide flat lands and . . . But sometimes, I just felt like I was—I don't know. Buried in all that space. Buried by all that openness, that emptiness. I just had to get out. I just had to. I used to run with the kids down at the mall and we'd—we'd buy makeup together and clothes when we could. We'd all go home and dress up and pretend we were movie stars and rock stars. I knew that that was what you were supposed to do. That you were supposed to pretend and then forget it, grow out of it, marry, settle down, the whole thing. I tried to do that. When I met Wally, I thought: here's my chance, a real chance to find the way of life I'm supposed to have, to be the things that I'm supposed to be. But I couldn't. I just couldn't. I felt bad about leaving him, just deserting him like that, but I just—" The skin of her cheeks tightened, her lips pressed against each other. She was fighting off tears. "I had to get out," she said again. "Only, when I finally did, it wasn't what I expected. It wasn't what I expected at all. No one was . . . friendly. No one was . . . helpful." She almost laughed. "There was no one to take care of me, I guess. Everyone acted as if . . . They acted like hungry people at a dinner where there isn't enough food. I went to audition after audition and, jeez-Louise, Mr. Wells—John—they wouldn't even let me talk for five minutes before they'd chase me off, call the next one on. And I worked so hard, I—" She shook her head. I watched her framed against the summer sky. That sky was darkening now, thickening with clouds. The thunder rolled again, closer. Georgia Stuart looked out the window wistfully. "Looks like the heat might break after all."

"It's about time," I said. I smoked and watched her. I watched her breasts rise and fall with her breathing. I thought about her lonely life in the big city. I thought about mine.

"When I met someone here . . . When I met someone worthwhile at long last . . ." she said. She could not go on for a moment.

"Paul Abingdon?" I said.

She faced me. "What?"

I waited. I waited for her to lie.

"No," she said. "No, not Paul. Allen Simon." I nodded. She was coming clean. "Allen was one of Paul's aides. I met him at this restaurant where I worked, and he was just so . . . so polite and . . . and regular . . . just like real folks . . ."

"But he was Susan Scott's guy," I said.

She smiled. She flushed. She lowered her eyes. "You get to know everything after a while, don't you?"

"I get the story," I said. "I'm a reporter. I told you that."

"Okay." She lifted her chin. "Okay. He was Susan Scott's guy. At least she thought so. She brought him into the restaurant where we worked and we just . . . got along, that's all. I mean, he told me that Susan didn't even like him all that much. He told me she was just hanging around him to meet interesting people. And to get his apartment, too, when he left town."

I smoked my cigarette thoughtfully. "But you got his apartment," I said. "And you met the interesting people."

She rolled her eyes. "Oh, yeah, great. Real interesting."

"Wally says you thought Abingdon was going to help your career."

Her voice broke. "He said he was!" She covered her mouth with her hand as if ashamed of the cry that had escaped it. "Oh, John, you must think I'm so horrible. You must think I—I use men to—to—but it happened step by step. It all seemed so . . . I don't know. It seemed *all right*, at the time. You know? Allen introduced me to Paul and Paul was sweet and polite and interested in my career and he said he was going to introduce me to all the right people and Allen didn't seem to mind at all . . . in fact, he started taking me to these parties . . . these private parties where he knew Paul would be, just so we could . . . get together . . ."

The thunder struck hard just as her tears started falling. I saw the glow of lightning flash in the northern sky. Georgia put her hands over her face. Her shoulders shook. I heard her sniffle. And when she turned to me and spoke her voice was filled with hurt and indignation.

"They used *me*!" she said. "They traded me off from one of them to another without my even knowing it. Like I was a piece of property. Like I was a *thing*. Do you know what that's like, John? To be treated like some sort of—of object? Like you're just a body, a piece of—of meat that's there for them to use the way they want to. It's like they're telling you you don't have a soul inside you, like you're—you're making life inconvenient for them if you pretend to have a soul. Do you know what that feels like to be treated that way?"

"No," I said.

I snuffed my cigarette in the ashtray on the coffee table. I put my hands in my pockets. I walked over to the bay. I stood over Georgia where she sat in the love seat. She looked up at me. The tears rolled down her bruised cheeks. The tears were transparent. She was not wearing makeup. She was just fresh and pretty all on her own. Being young could do that for you.

I took one hand from my pocket, reached out and touched her hair. She trembled. She cried.

"Is that the truth?" I said.

"What?" She turned her head. She pressed her cheek against the palm of my hand.

"Is that really the way it was?"

"I swear. I swear. I just . . . I just want to go home," she said. The words were muffled as her lips brushed my hand.

"I want to help you, Georgia, but if you lie to me now—"

"It's all true. I swear."

"How many times did you sleep with Paul Abingdon?"

She covered my hand with her own as she moved against it. "Once. Just once."

"Where?"

"I—what, I—in an apartment. Downtown somewhere. He said it belonged to a friend. April something—I—I don't remember her other name."

"Did you suspect there was someone there? The photographer?"

"No. I only heard about the pictures a week or so later. Paul called me . . . he thought I was trying to blackmail him. He wouldn't believe me. Those men, those men last night, they must have thought that, too. They all . . . Oh, I don't know . . . Everyone else . . ."

Her voice trailed off. "What?" I said.

"Are you my friend, Mr. Wells? I don't have anyone else. Are you my friend?"

"I've got to write the story, Georgia. That's what I do. I've got to."

She shook her head a little. I felt it against my palm. "Oh, I don't care. I don't care about that anymore. It's just: when those men took me last night. Those terrible men . . . When they hurt me . . . And then, when you came for me, and fought for me like that, I just thought . . . I just thought: finally. Finally."

She took hold of my arm and drew herself out of the love seat. We were face to face. I watched her lips moving as she spoke to me.

"I've been so scared. Even before last night. When that man was killed, the man with the pictures, I hoped it was over, I prayed and prayed it would be over, and when you showed up, I hoped I could get you to go away, to leave it alone."

She brought my hand back up to her cheek. I tried to tug it away. She held on. I watched her.

"The woman who came to me today," she said. "The woman from Paul's office. She said if I didn't leave town, Paul would tell lies about me."

"Yeah," I told her softly. "He does that."

"She said Paul would say I tried to blackmail him, that I arranged to have the pictures taken."

"I can believe it."

"She said I might have to go to jail, that it would be my word against a congressman's. Oh God." She sobbed once. "I'm so glad you came back. I'm so glad you found me again . . ."

She stepped toward me. She tilted her face up to mine. Her breath was warm.

"Stop it," I said—but I said it hoarsely. "You've been used enough."

"I'm glad you found me," she repeated, defiant.

"You're too young. You could be my daughter, Georgia."

"That's no reason. That's no reason for us to lose each other, John. I won't let you lose me because of that."

Her face swam closer to me. Her breath grew hot. I kissed her lightly on the lips before I even knew I had. And then I kissed her again more deeply.

"Don't leave me. You're all I've got," she said.

I pulled her close to me and kissed her for a long, long time. I'd been wrong. All wrong about the need dying and the hunger dying.

They do not die. They never die.

24

I was awakened by the rain. It hit hard when it finally hit. I opened my eyes to see it washing in sheets against the high mullioned windows in Georgia's bedroom. For a moment, I did not know the time or the day or where I was. The room was in shadow. The sky was darker than it had been before but the long summer day had not yet ended. It felt odd to be in bed in the afternoon.

I remembered all at once. I sat up, startled. Looked around me. The bed was large and soft. I was alone in it. I heard a noise, raised my eyes and saw a door, the bathroom door. A thin strip of light was showing underneath it. A shadow was moving in that light.

I relaxed. I found my cigarettes on the bedside table. I lit one. I propped myself against the headboard. I sat gazing at the window across the room. Thunder banged loudly all around me. The rain slapped into the pane again and again. Lightning lit the droplets as they tumbled down it. I smoked my cigarette and watched the storm that had come at last.

And I thought about Georgia. I thought about the long, slow hour of her and the feverish minutes. My hands remembered her nakedness.

There was the sound of running water. I turned to the bathroom door. It snapped open. I saw her silhouetted, still naked, in the light. The sight of her held me silent. The curve of her breasts, of her hips. She killed the light behind her and stepped forward into the bedroom shadows. She

ame to the bed. She sat on the edge of it. The lightning
barked beyond the window. The thunder crashed. The
ain kept up a rhythmic whisper, loud, then softer, then
oud again.

"You're awake," said Georgia.

"Yeah."

"I didn't know whether to wake you."

"Is it late? Have I been out long?"

"No. Only twenty minutes or so. It's only six-thirty or
. You have time."

I reached for her. I lay my hand on her thigh. The smooth-
ess, the resilience—I almost thought I had imagined them.

"You're so young," I said.

She laughed. "Do you like that?"

"Yes," I said.

"Oh, I'll bet."

I laughed. "It was great."

"*You're* great."

"I'm old."

"You're old and great," said Georgia. She reached under
he sheet and touched my thigh. "You're still great."

"And still old. Careful, or you'll wind up in the *Enquirer*.
cantily clad woman drags herself out from under dead
ver."

"Stop that." She giggled.

"No, it's true, it's a condition I have. Too much bliss
nd—" I snapped my fingers.

She giggled some more. I laid my cigarette in an ashtray.
pulled her to me. I kissed her. She kept her hand beneath
he sheet.

"You don't feel dead," she said.

"Not yet."

She pulled away from me. She stood up.

"Where're you going?"

"I'm going to get dressed."

"Come back."

"I can't. We're late."

I groaned. "For what?"

"Your deadline, dopey. You forget? I won't have y
saying I seduced you to get you to drop this story."

She moved to a dresser on the wall with the windo
She was lit by the gray light of the storm. The shadows
raindrops streaked her back. She opened a drawer, be
over and rummaged in it. I studied her. She looked ba
at me over her shoulder. "You thought about that, did
you?"

"Don't move," I said. "You're beautiful."

"Hmm. You did, though. I know." She straightened w
a pair of panties in her hands. She slipped them on.

I sighed. I sat up on the edge of the bed. All in all, I f
well satisfied.

"Say, how old are you anyway?" I said.

She was slipping a bra on now. "Just never mind."

"I mean, this isn't the most professional thing I've ev
done here . . . Are you legal at least?"

"John!"

"Well, I feel like an old . . . you know . . . whatever–

"Lecher's the word you're looking for, and you are."

There was a lamp standing on the bedside table. I turn
it on. I caught her just as she raised a light dress above h
head. Then the dress came down. She tugged it straig
around her. She threw back her chestnut hair. She saw ▮
watching her.

"What are you thinking about over there?" she asked m

I shook my head, and did not answer. I had been thinki
about Lansing.

My clothes were lying in a heap on the floor. I plant
my cigarette in my mouth again as I tugged on my unde
wear and my pants. I stood up. I buckled my belt. Cigare
smoke gathered around my face and I squinted through

I stood still and it was quiet in the room except for t
wash and whisper of the rain.

And then I knew that she had lied to me. That all of it had been a lie.

It hit me that way. It hit me suddenly like that. But even as it hit me, I knew it was not all that sudden, not really. I knew it had been there for some long time under the loneliness and the lust and the loss of Lansing. But now, with the hunger satisfied, it swam quickly to the surface and I could not deny it anymore.

I felt the blood drain from my face. I glanced at Georgia. She was looking into a makeup mirror atop the dresser. She was brushing her hair.

"Why did they come for you?" I asked her.

She heard the strangeness of my voice. The brush stopped moving. She kept looking at the mirror. But I saw her eyes—she was looking past her own reflection, at me.

She laughed. "What . . . ? Who?"

"Marino. Dellacroce's men. Why did they think you had the pictures?"

"I . . ." The smile was frozen on her lips. "They said they followed you . . . I . . ."

Then I was behind her. I had her by the shoulders. I spun her around. She cried out, her hair flying. I forced her to confront me.

"John!" she said.

"Look at me."

"John, why are you—"

"Look at me!" My voice rasped deep in my throat. "You can't be that good. No one's that good. You can't be."

Her face came around to me. Her sweet, fresh face. It was expressionless. Her soft, brown eyes seemed flat. I could see nothing beyond the surface of them.

Then she smiled. Just slightly. Just at one corner of her mouth. She tilted her head and she smiled at me almost coyly.

"That good?" she said. "Why—I'm going to be one of the greats."

I was afraid of her suddenly, and I let her go. I backed away a step.

"Kendrick was *your* man, wasn't he? Sure he was. He was working with you. Marino would have known that. He would have had his eye on Kendrick because of the hooked ring. When he finally killed him and the pictures turned up missing, it was only natural he would come to you: you were Kendrick's partner."

She shrugged. "Poor Mayforth. He was a little scumbag, but he had his uses. He saw I was in with Abingdon's crowd and he thought there could be money in it."

I didn't answer. I felt the chill of her voice deep in my flesh. I had caressed her, kissed her—I had been inside her not an hour ago. I recoiled another step. I met her smile with a wild rictus of my own.

She made a face. "Oh, well, why not, John? I mean, really. Why shouldn't I have gotten something out of it? Simon and Abingdon were passing me around like I was some little tart, weren't they? They thought I was just a country girl who didn't know what they were doing. Well, I just let them think that. I played it that way. But I knew. I knew, all right. And I'm *not* a tart. I'm *not* some little whore for them to fuck and forget and pass around—" For a moment, as I had in the car the other night, I looked in her eyes and took the fathomless measure of her rage. Then it was gone from view. "I'm an actress," she finished coolly.

"Yeah," I said. "Yeah, you are. But what did you need me for?"

"Sorry, Johnny, that's the way it goes."

"No really. Where did I come into it? Why did Kendrick come to me? I mean, if Abingdon's paid you off now, he have paid you off then. Wouldn't he?"

She nodded slyly, eyeing me sideways. "Uh-huh."

Then it hit me. My lips parted. I tried to speak. I tried again. "You wanted the ink," I said. "You wanted the money—but you also wanted the ink."

She threw back her head and her laugh trilled like a bird.

ng. "It was a good idea, anyway. A little scandal. Get the
ll rolling. I mean, what the fuck, you know, John?"

"Sure. Sure, what the fuck. And the *Star* was perfect.
e might not have paid as much as the magazines, but we
ouldn't have printed the real raw stuff either. Just enough
turn the public on. Just enough to make them want more.
fter that, who knows what the magazines would have paid?"

"Sure beats the hell out of auditioning," she said.

For a moment, in the chill of her voice, in the quiet
uelty of her smile, in the memory of my hands upon her
d our bodies together, the world seemed so jumbled that
could not make sense of anything. "Mrs. Abingdon told
e today she wasn't going to let her husband's career be
ined by a blackmailer. . . ."

Now Georgia's smile broadened. Now it was a full, bright
hio smile. "Mrs. Abingdon is an uptight little cunt," she
id. "She doesn't know shit."

"I thought she meant Kendrick. She meant you. You went
them after Kendrick was killed, but . . . where were the
ctures? I mean, even if you had them . . ."

She shrugged again, sighed. "I didn't need them. Abing-
n knows that whoever has them can't come forward any-
ore. It'd be like confessing to murder. All I needed to do
as promise to stay out of town." She snorted a little. "And
u know what's funny?" she asked me. "What's funny is:
d have done it before, if you hadn't come along. I was
ing to go the minute Kendrick got offed. Then, you came
ound and, at first, I figured I'd put you off until I could
ach Abingdon, but then I started thinking: why not? You
ow? I mean, really, when it comes down to it, I'd rather
ve the press than the money. And now with the pictures
ne—"

"With the pictures gone, you could tell the story any way
u wanted," I said. "But then what? What happened then?
id Dellacroce make it too dangerous? Marino scare you
?"

Her smile faded. Her hand moved up to touch the bruises

on her cheek. "He hurt my face," she said. "I can't aff
that. My body is my instrument—"

"So you went back to plan A. Stalled me and went
Abingdon. He must have figured he could buy me off
and end it there. But I wouldn't play. I came after you

She gestured blithely. "So now I get the money *and*
story."

"Only now it's my story—told my way."

She tilted her head to one side. "You're not that stup
Wells," she said. "You're stupid. But you're not that s
pid."

"No, hell. Hell, I'm smart. I've suddenly gotten v
smart." I kept my eyes on her as I moved back to the p
of clothing on the floor. I picked up my shirt and pulled
on. I started to button it quickly. My gaze drifted. I look
past her. At the window. At the rain. "Yeah," I said. "N
that the heat is off, I'm brilliant. Now that I've had yo
I'm a regular brain trust."

Georgia shrugged again. "Some women have that effe
dearest. They're beautiful until the moment you get the
then suddenly you notice you're lying on top of a real witc
She laughed. It was the same laugh of a moment befo
fresh and lively, vibrant, young. But there was anoth
sound mingling with it now, another sound lying just b
neath it. It was not the sound of her cruelty. Not even t
sound of her red-hot rage. It was the sound instead o
terrible emptiness: it was her sound, her final sound. "B
you're a little old to believe in witches, aren't you?" s
said. She laughed again.

"No," I said. "Just old enough."

Her tone grew thick with pity. "Oh, poor man. Did y
get fooled by the bad lady?"

"Don't flatter yourself." I sat on the edge of the bed
collected my cigarettes from the table. I pushed my sh
on. "I did that job for you."

"You guys always do," Georgia sang out on a note

riumph. And then with relish: "You make acting so easy.
You turn me into something in your own dear little heads
and then all I have to do is pretend that that's what I am
and . . . bingo. You'll do anything. Anything. Paul Abingdon wants all the little girls to bow down and worship him,
so he figures they must all want to, also. All I did was play
along and until the moment he was satisfied, he would have
sold his soul for me. That's the way it works. The moment
you fellows have had it, all your fantasies go back into your
pants pockets and you toss the real thing away like garbage.
But sometimes by then . . . it's too late."

I was still sitting on the bed. Just sitting there now. Just
sitting and staring at her. The sight of her—still with that
little smile, still with those hard, flat eyes—it made my
heart feel like ashes: chill, gray.

"What about Wally Shakespeare?" I asked her. "I'm just
curious. What about him?"

"He wanted someone to redeem," she said.

"Yeah, but . . . what was in it for you?"

She made a loose gesture. "Oh, it was just a bet I made
with my friends. They said I couldn't get him to do it. I
won the last few dollars I needed for my stake to New York."

I nodded. I stood. My jacket was flung over a chair. I
picked it up, tossed it over my shoulder. I walked around
the bed until I was standing right in front of her. She grinned
at me, lifting her chin, sticking her chest out as if she were
daring me to hit her.

"And what about you, Johnny?" she said. "Who was I to
you?"

I stared into that freckled midwestern face for a long
moment. "Nothing fancy, kid," I told her. "Just someone
I know."

I kept walking. I walked to the door.

"And just where are we off to now?" she called after me.

I paused in the doorway, turned to her. "To the *Star*.
I'm on deadline, remember?"

"Oh yes. I remember," she said. "But be careful now
Johnny. If you write nasty things about me, I'm going t
say some very nasty things about you. Like that I neve
slept with Paul Abingdon—but that I did sleep with you
That you made the Abingdon story up just to blackmail m
into bed with you . . . oh, there's any number of things
can say now. All sorts of things that will make perfect sens
to everyone—and believe me, I'll have plenty of person;
details to back them up. You go back to your newspape
Johnny, you go back and write your story. But you write
my way. The way I told it to you. You write it my way, (
I'll show you just what newspapers can do to a person if h
violates the great moral code."

I went for her. She tried to hit me with her brush.
knocked it out of her hands. I grabbed the front of her dre;
in my fist. She spit in my face. I slapped her. Her hea
snapped back. She was quiet. She glared at me, her lij
drawn up, her teeth showing.

"You think you're high pressure, Ohio? You're amatei
night," I said. "I've had the big monkeys on my back sinc
this story began and I'll tell you what: I'm sick of it. I don
care what Bush wants or Dellacroce wants or Abingdon (
you. I'm gonna write this story my way. I'm a reporter
That's what I do with stories. I get them and I write then
You wanted ink, sister? I'm gonna give you ink. I'm gonn
drown you in it."

I tossed her back against the dresser. I turned and walke
out of the room.

"It's too late for that, Wells!" she shouted after me.

I went out the front door into the hall. She came int
the living room behind me.

"You got what you wanted out of me," she said, "an
now the bill's due. You're gonna pay just like everybod
else. Everybody pays, Wells!"

I started down the stairs. She followed me out the doo
She stood on the landing above me.

"You write that shit about me, Wells, and you're through. I swear it. I'll finish you. I'll finish you but good."

She was still yelling at me when I reached the ground floor. Maybe she was still yelling when I stepped outside, but by then her voice was swept away by the steady patter of the rain.

25

Hammered by thunder, slashed by lightning, the rain came down hard. It stood like a curtain of running silver between the eye and the city. Everything faded into a blur behind it.

I stumbled down the stoop, barely able to see. I kept my chin tucked in, my collar pulled up around me. By the time I reached the corner of Irving, I was soaked. My hair was plastered to my head. My jacket hung heavy on me. I plunged down the street against the current, gasping at the blow of the water. I found the Artful Dodge and wrestled the door open. I tumbled inside, sopping. I sat behind the wheel, catching my breath, spitting rain.

The rain pounded on the old Dart's roof. I started the engine. I slapped a cigarette between my teeth and lit it. The windshield was completely awash. I could see nothing through it but the shifting patterns of the water. I started the wipers. They shoved the patterns away but the rain fell too fast for them. The view was still obscured, still out of focus.

I pulled out and drove slowly to Gramercy, then out to Third. I headed uptown, leaning forward against the wheel, peering through the glass at the fuzzy glow of streetlights and stoplights, and the gray haze of the road underneath.

It took all my attention. I could not think. Not until I got to a red light. Then I stopped. Then I thought. I did not like it much. It was not pleasant.

I was finished. I was through. By the time Monday came, I would not have a job in the newspaper business. I was not sure I ever would again. Even Bush couldn't have done that to me. Guys like that are powerful, but they're not all-powerful. With my clips, my reputation, I'd have gotten a job somewhere no matter what he'd done. Abingdon, too, congressman that he was—he couldn't have ruined me like this either. He might have lied his head off trying, but he'd have gotten caught up eventually. Dellacroce, Marino—they could have killed me. They might still. But I had a lot of friends in the business, and a lot more on the police force. A smart guy like Dellacroce, just out of jail, would tend to discipline his own troops, and let me be.

None of them could have ruined me like this, taken my work away from me. Not even Georgia. Not even her with all her plotting, all her acting. She could not have pulled this little triumph off alone. She needed help.

She needed help from me. Only I could have gotten myself into this fine mess. Looking in the wrong place for the wrong woman. Running too hard from the things that hurt and matter.

Lansing was right. I had it in for myself but good. I hadn't even left myself a way out.

Smart girl, Lansing. That guy—the one who was rich and handsome and brilliant and young—he was lucky too.

The light turned green. I pushed on up Third through the rain.

I, on the other hand, was out of luck. Definitely. Finally. I had my story and I was going to write it. But with both Georgia and Abingdon denying it, and with Georgia revealing that she'd slept with me, it was not going to stand up too well. No. Only the photographs themselves would save me now, and they were evidence of a murder, not likely to show up soon.

The wipers swept to one side. I saw the light on the corner of Thirtieth turn yellow. It went dim as it was covered by the rain. The wipers brought it clear again. I slowed the car. Stopped as the light turned red. I took my cigarette from my lips. I smelled my fingers through the smell of smoke. They smelled of her. Of Georgia.

I thought: *If Marino doesn't have the pictures and Georgia doesn't, and she hasn't sold them to Abingdon, then where the hell are they?*

Not that many people really knew the pictures existed. Georgia did. I did. Abingdon probably found out about them on the news like everybody else. So it was me and Georgia and Marino and Kendrick himself.

The light turned green. I barely noticed it. I kept my foot on the brake. The car stood still. Another car went around me to the right. One went by me to the left. Then there was a lull as I sat there, thinking. The windshield wipers whisked and squeaked. The rain tattooed the roof.

But then maybe there was someone else, I thought. Someone else who knew about the photos. Someone Georgia or Kendrick told.

A car honked loudly. A truck let fly with his bullhorn. I roused myself and pulled the Dodge to the side.

Blackmailers. Mrs. Abingdon had said she would not let her husband be ruined by some dime-store blackmailers. More than one. Georgia approached them for hush money after her run-in with Marino. But what about Kendrick? Maybe he'd gone into business for himself. Maybe when I turned down the photos, he figured the only way he'd make real money was to blackmail the candidate, sell them to Abingdon. But then Kendrick would have blabbed about it when Marino came to call.

Unless Marino hadn't killed him. Maybe Georgia paid the call to Kendrick. Maybe she did sell the pictures to Abingdon . . .

I rolled down the window. I stuck my head out. I was soaked by the steady downpour as I looked back down Third Avenue. The traffic coming up was sparse. I waited for an opening. I pulled out and ran the Dodge up the avenue to Thirty-second. I made a right and slogged through the gathering flood to Second. Turned right again at the corner. Rolled downtown. Back to Georgia's.

The thunder seemed directly overhead now. It pounded

like a fist on the rooftops of Manhattan. The lightning made long jagged streaks connecting heaven and the skyscrapers. The rain beat down on the cars, on the buildings, on the pavement. It beat down in wave after wave.

The light, what light was left, was dying as I reached Gramercy again. Behind those black clouds, the sun was falling. The rain had changed from streaks of silver to sheets of gray. The day seemed to fold in upon itself, narrowing down to a dark center of oncoming night and the rain.

I double parked across the street from Georgia's building. I turned on my flashers. I pulled up my collar. I stepped out into the storm.

I came around the Dodge. A Volks came trundling down the street. I waited for it to pass so I could cross. I looked up at Georgia's building.

I saw it through the water and through the haze of dusk. I saw the bay window. I saw the streaks of rain on the glass.

There was an electric snap. The pane went white. I saw a fork of lightning reflected on it. It died and I saw Georgia standing there, standing in the bay with her back to me.

The thunder came. A great clap that shook me. Georgia seemed to float closer to me as I watched. She seemed to become magnified behind the rain on the window. Then the window itself seemed to enlarge and expand.

The lightning flashed again. The window shattered. Georgia Stuart tumbled backward into the downpour. She fell four stories, her body turning and turning in the air.

She struck the sidewalk as the thunder struck. Her body bounced a little. It rocked. It settled. I ran across the street toward her. As I came on, I saw the blood begin to run out onto the pavement from beneath her head. It ran thickly, a broad pool of it, deep red. And then it grew thinner, and the color lightened to pink.

And then it was washed away completely by the rain.

26

I knelt beside her. She was staring up at me, up into my eyes. She was not pretty anymore. The fall had bruised and broken her.

But it had not killed her. She was dead all right, but she had died as she staggered back through the window. Died of the bullet that made her stagger when it drilled its hole in the center of her forehead.

The rain that pounded on my back dampened her hair, plastered it to the pavement around her. It washed her face, rinsed the blood from it in rivulets until the hole in her brow stood out naked, black and jagged. I hurt, looking at her, as if her flesh and mine were still connected.

I looked up and down the street for help. There was no one in sight. Not even a car passed under the sycamores. The sycamores waved and bowed and trembled under the storm. I was alone with them.

And then the door to the brownstone opened.

The killer was a shadow. He was hidden by the downpour. He stood at the top of the stoop and I could only make out the shape of him through the darkness and through the silver rain that streaked the darkness. I could see him pause there, stone still, as if stunned. I could see him hunch his shoulders, hang his head. I could see the shape of the long-barreled gun that dangled loosely from the hand hanging at his side.

He came forward. He descended to the sidewalk step by step. The rain drenched my face as I looked up at him. I blinked and gasped. He turned—to see her one more time, I think. Only then did he notice me. He moved toward me slowly until his features were clear. I already knew who he was from the outline of him. But he seemed surprised to see me.

He licked his lips. He brought his free hand up to brush the damp hair from his forehead. The sky lit up above us. Thunder struck.

"Mr. Wells?" he said.

I sighed. I stood up. "Wally."

We faced each other across the body of the murdered girl. He stared at me, waiting for me to speak. I could not think of anything to say.

"I came to bring mercy," Wally Shakespeare said, "but I had to bring justice instead."

"Why?" I shouted it above the storm. "Why the hell did you have to do that?"

He gazed down at her. He shook his head. "She wasn't pure," he told me, disappointed.

I closed my eyes a moment. I nodded slowly. I understood.

I wanted to be angry at him. I wasn't. I was just sad. I felt for him with his dream of her, and for me with mine. And I felt for her, with her dream to be in the dreams of millions.

"I came here tonight to forgive her," said Wally. "I explained that to Susan. That's why Susan told me, finally, where she lived. I came to forgive her for the weakness of all women. Since Eve, Mr. Wells. I knew when I first saw that terrible man with his terrible pictures, I knew he was the serpent in the garden. I knew what I had to do." The rain poured down his cheeks. I couldn't tell it from the tears. "But I would have forgiven *her*!" he cried. "And then I came here and she was with another man."

I closed my eyes. I heard the thunder crash. Not as loudly as before. It was moving on.

"I saw them," Wally said, "I saw them together through

the window of her room. So I waited. I waited till I saw him leave. It was raining so hard by then, I couldn't even make out his face. I don't even know what he looked like."

I stared up at him. "Why didn't you kill him, too?"

"Him?" he said, surprised. "It wasn't his fault. He was . . . he was tempted . . . by Eve. The devil tempts the woman. The woman tempts the man. That's how it works."

"Oh," I said. I'd always wondered how it worked. Now I knew.

His eyes were wide. "Everything that is impure," he explained to me, "infects everything else. It seduces everybody else. It makes us desire it. That's why we have to get rid of it—of impurity—wherever we find it. We have to snuff it out before it pulls us in. Pollutes us. That's why nothing can be left alone that is not pure or we're all done for. Do you understand? Do you understand now?"

He leaned toward me, eager-eyed. The pistol patted impatiently against his thigh. I wanted to say something. I really did. Standing there in the midst of that torrent. Standing there with Georgia lying twisted and dead on the pavement between us, I wanted to say: She had it right, my friend. We made her what she was. She seduced us because we wanted her to. We wanted her to, so we turned her into what we loved. Listen to me, I wanted to say, listen to me because I understand. If she deceived us, if she was impure, it was because she let the image of our need dance over her like a mirror. But that was no reason to kill her. Better to take a good long look at the reflection she was showing you. Better to get to know that need and know it well. Otherwise, you can curse her all you want, you can gun her down a hundred times, and it's still a good chance you'll wake up one morning in bed with her, in some bed, anyway, with someone like her, some bed you made yourself the night before and all the nights before.

I wanted to say that. But it was late. We all had things to do. I figured I'd let it pass.

Anyway, Wally Shakespeare wasn't listening now. He was

azing off into the distance, into the lightning flashes on
he far sky. His mind was on God knows what mission of
urity and judgment.

"Well," he said, and the thunder and the patter of the
ain nearly drowned him out. "Well, I've got to go now."

He stepped forward. He stepped over the body of Geor-
ia Stuart. He lumbered by me, the pistol at his side. I
urned and followed his progress. He headed down the
treet into the shadows under the trees. Soon, the rain
bscured him. The darkness swallowed him. He was gone.

27

That was the worst of the heat, I remember. The rain pret
much broke the back of it. August ended mild, and the
was a chill in the air of September. After Labor Day, t
temperature did not touch eighty again.

By then, of course, the election was in full swing. Abin
don wasn't a candidate anymore. He'd stepped down an
been replaced on the ticket by a state assemblyman name
George Kelly. George was nothing special, but no one cou
find anything wrong with him either. At the end of Octobe
he was running ahead in the polls by several lengths.

It seemed pretty clear he was going to beat Christi
Maldonado, at any rate. Old Mr. M.'s campaign faltere
grievously after my series linking him to Marino and De
lacroce hit the stands. In October, too, Alphonse Mari
himself turned up in the trunk of an '84 Cadillac. His han
and feet had been tied together and his head had bee
blown apart. Many political observers took this to me
that Maldonado had lost his base of support. The candida
never did concede defeat but that didn't seem to matt
much to anyone but him.

All that, though, was at election time, when an old r
porter's fancy turns to thoughts of selling insurance for
living. All that came later, in the fall.

It was Georgia Stuart's death that night that seemed
end the summer for me, and the long dearth of news th
marked the summer. Her death did a lot of things for m
in fact. It got me off the hook. Saved my career, my re

tation, probably my life. When she died, I got a story that
ould put the *Star* on top of the Abingdon scandal for good.
didn't have to worry that she would try to discredit me
y lying—or even telling the truth—about our hour to-
ether. And, her murder led the cops to search through
Wally Shakespeare's luggage, a search that turned up the
ell-thumbed pictures of Georgia and Abingdon to prove
y word was good. Finally, with Georgia dead, with the
ull story told, Dellacroce had no real reason to send his
oons after me anymore. He was unlikely to chance hitting
reporter just to save face.

So all in all, I did pretty well on Georgia's murder. I'm
ot proud of it, but that's the way it is. You can't get involved
ith a dirty little story without getting dirty yourself. Hell,
aybe you wouldn't get involved at all, if you didn't have
ome of the dirt on you to begin with.

All things considered, then, maybe I should have been
rateful to Wally Shakespeare for killing his girl. Maybe it
as thankless of me to call the police on him. But I did.
s soon as he moved off into the rain that night, I left
eorgia's side. I shouldered through the storm to the pay
hone on the corner. I called the cops first. Then I called
e paper. I got Harriet Coleman, an assistant city editor.

"Hello, sweetheart, get me rewrite," I said.

"Who is this?"

"Wells."

"Stop kidding around, Wells, we're on deadline. Jesus."

"Well, hold page one."

"Kiss my ass."

"I mean it. You know the girl in the Abingdon photos?"

"The imaginary girl in the imaginary photos?"

"Yeah," I said. "She's got an imaginary bullet hole in her
maginary head, I know who the imaginary killer is, and if
ou don't give me a rewrite man, you're going to have an
naginary job."

She laughed. "I can't believe this. You're serious. You
eally want me to remake page one and get you rewrite."

"I even called you sweetheart."

"God, this is great. Wait till I tell my husband. Hold o
I'll pass you on to McKay."

So I told my story to McKay and he wrote it for me.
wasn't everything, not yet. But it was more than anyo
else would have for hours to come. Later, with Gottlie
help, I pieced together the rest of it. How Georgia h
come to New York and adopted the stage name of Ap
Thomas. How she quickly grew weary of the cold, cr
world of the New York theater. She was probably mo
than ready for a change of pace when Allen Simon from th
Abingdon campaign came into her life. Georgia must ha
realized pretty fast that he had two things she could us
connections, and an apartment. The apartment turned o
to be by far the more useful of the two. A move to a mo
elegant location could only help her in her career, and
would help her avoid Wally, too, who had phoned her fro
California by then. But after she hooked into Abingd
himself, the move seemed positively inspired. Delilal
Kendrick's girlfriend, told me that Georgia offered her o
apartment to Kendrick as a base of operations for his ne
business enterprise. In return, all he had to do was take
couple of photographs and peddle them to the press. N
money down and instant celebrity for Georgia Stuart, who
decided, by that time, that her old name would do just fin
When Kendrick got killed, Marino got the story from D
lilah and told her to keep her mouth shut. She did.

So Kendrick moved into Georgia's apartment—and tha
when Wally showed up. He came looking for his girl a
found Kendrick instead. Kendrick laughed at him, told hi
that Georgia didn't want to see him. When that didn't tak
Kendrick, still laughing, showed him the pictures. Kendri
was laughing still when Wally pulled out his dad's old cro
shooter and, with many a biblical remonstrance, blew o
the little pimp's brains.

That last part of it was in Wally's confession. The co
got it out of him the very night he killed the girl he love

fter they came and got Georgia's body and talked to me,
hey put out a call for him. Rounded him up in Times Square
ot an hour later. He was standing in the rain underneath
he news zipper on the Number One tower. He was preach-
ng to the storm, waving his gun in the air, shouting fire
nd brimstone over the lightning and thunder. Above him,
belt of electric letters carried word of the day's events
round and around.

We got the arrest into the final edition. The *Daily News*
an a brief on it, too, but they did not have the link to
bingdon. After that, I stuck with it just to make sure
othing slipped by me. I hung out with the police until
idnight or so and then came back to the office to write
p my notes.

Around seven the next morning, I was awakened by a
entle prodding at my shoulder. I opened my eyes to find
y cheek resting against the cold, hard top plate of my
)lympia. I raised my head and blinked up into the face of
ansing.

"I figured I'd find you here," she said softly. She smiled.

She'd brought me coffee and a bagel. She rolled a chair
p to my cubicle door and watched me eat. Behind her,
he city room's maze of white partitions stood silent. I saw
janitor pushing a vacuum against the far wall.

"You still talking to me?" Lansing asked me.

"Yeah, hell, more or less," I said around a mouthful.
Why are you here so early anyway?"

"Couldn't sleep."

I nodded. I sipped my coffee. I ate my bagel.

"Thinking," she said.

I nodded. I sipped. "You know what I've been thinking
bout?" I said.

She looked down at the tips of her shoes. She shook her
ead. I watched her hair whip back and forth.

"I've been wondering," I said, "why Bush let me get
way with this. After I insulted him and all. Why'd he give
ne a chance to get this story? Why didn't he just fire me?"

She looked up at me from under lowered brows. H
mouth turned upward at the corners. The story of my mee
ing with the people upstairs was all over the city room
now. "Is that really what you've been thinking about?"

"Yeah, off and on. Among other things. You know."
sipped. I ate.

"I'll tell you what I've heard," said Lansing.

"Okay."

"I've heard our friend Cambridge has had it. I've hea
he's through at the *Star*."

"Come on," I said. "Wishful thinking."

"Maybe," said Lansing. "But Bush must have had som
thing in mind when he gave you a chance like that. I figu
he's been listening to Cambridge beef about you long enoug
he decided it was time to see for himself who was righ
When Cambridge made this play to get rid of you, Bus
decided to set the two of you off against each other. If yo
didn't come through, you would have been out. The w
it is, I think Cambridge better start looking for anoth
paper to relate to."

I shook my head. "Office politics. It's all too complicate
for me."

She made a face. "I'll bet."

I polished off the bagel. I lit a cigarette. Lansing watche
me with her blue, blue eyes. I watched her back. I sipp
my coffee. I smoked.

"I'm sorry," she said. "I'm sorry I've been giving yo
such a hard—"

"What's it like out?" I asked her.

"What?"

"Is it still raining?"

"Oh. No. No, blue skies all over. Brand new day. B
listen—"

"Hot, though?"

She shook her head. "Around eighty. Not humid. Ve
nice."

I nodded. I smoked. I drained the coffee.

"I'm not gonna marry him," said Lansing.

"Who?"

"Wells!"

I laughed. "Okay."

She took a deep breath. "I don't love him," she said. "So
'm not going to marry him and that's it. My mother is just
oing to have to live with it."

I smoked. "Okay," I said.

"I wanted to tell you. I wanted you to know I decided
hat."

"Okay."

"But, I mean, it's my decision. It's what I want. No one
lse is to blame."

"Okay," I said.

"But I may be a pain for a while. I may be cantankerous."

"Lansing," I said, "you're always cantankerous."

She reared back in her chair. "I am not. When am I
antankerous?"

"All the time. You're always a pain, too."

"Well, what do you think you are, my friend?"

"Tired," I said. "I'm tired. I need another cup of coffee."
stood up. "Wanna come? We'll go over to the terminal,
vatch the rush."

"Okay." She stood in front of me. She looked up at me.
All at once, her expression grew soft. Her eyes opened up
n a depth of sorrow. Her lips were pursed and her body
eemed to lean toward me in a silent appeal.

"Stop looking at me like that, Lansing," I whispered.

Then I put my hand against her cheek. For a long time,
ve stood there silently.

ABOUT THE AUTHOR

KEITH PETERSON is a radio and newspaper journalist who lives in New York City. He is the author of three John Wells mysteries: *The Trapdoor, There Fell a Shadow* and *The Rain. The Scarred Man*, a novel of psychological suspense to be published by Bantam in early 1989, has been sold to the movies. Under a pseudonym, he is an Edgar Award–winning author.